THOSE LITTLE BASTARDS

BOOKS BY CLARK

THE STAINS OF TIME

The Piano of Death
The Boot of Destiny
The Chains of Desire
The Elixir of Denial
The Dance of Dreams

OTHER BOOKS

Those Little Bastards
All He Left Behind
Missing Mr. Wingfield
The Seven Wives of Silver
Bad Poetry Night
Out of the Woods
Under the World

THOSE LITTLE BASTARDS

E. CHRISTOPHER CLARK

First published in 2002 by
Clarkwoods Press
Dracut, Massachusetts

Second Edition published in 2014 by
Clarkwoods LLC
Merrimack, New Hampshire

ISBN for the Print Edition: 978-1-952044-00-7
ISBN for the Digital Edition: 978-1-952044-01-4

Library of Congress Control Number: 2002094344

PREFACE

The stories in this book were first written between 1995 and 2002, when I was between the ages of 18 and 25. That version of me had a much narrower worldview and far less sensitivity to the way my words might trigger the traumatized. My tendency to challenge readers with difficult material had yet to be tempered by the core desire I have now, in late 2023, to do no harm.

I have considered pulling this book from publication altogether, but the Internet never truly lets something disappear. And so, I've done what I can to lessen any hurt the book might inadvertently cause by adding this brief preface and the following mea culpas:

- "Ezekiel and the Harvesters" contains many stereotypes of the Amish. I regret I did not do more research here.
- "Hacker" depicts an incident of catfishing which leads to rape by deception. The intent of the story, when written in the mid-90s, was to depict the potential horrors of online dating. I could have written it far

more sensitively and without the same level of sexual violence.

- "Out of the Groove" contains another depiction of rape by deception. Here, our protagonist pretends to be her well-known twin sister so that she can hook up with a guy she's into. Everyone seems to enjoy themselves and the truth comes out in a far less violent way than in "Hacker," but it's still technically rape by deception. I would not use this plot element today.
- "The Perfect Pitch" includes a sexual relationship between a teacher and student. Both are adults, but the student is significantly younger than the teacher. If I explored such a plot element today, I would do so far more carefully.

Thank you for taking the time to read this preface. I hope, despite these issues, you can get something out of the book—even if it's just a list of things *not* to do in your own writing.

E. Christopher Clark
Chelmsford, Massachusetts
December 14, 2023

CONTENTS

For Mom & Dad, who let me roam the yard talking to myself; and Stephanie, who never questioned this was what I was meant to do

❧ I ❧
A LITTLE OLD LADY IN
THE MACHINE OF GOD

REVELATION

E mily got out of bed at eight A.M. By then, she'd fallen in and out of sleep at least six times. It had been that way for her ever since her stroke. Sleeping was tedious, as horrible a chore at ninety-five as getting up on time had been at twenty. It just took away from things. It was a bother, more or less. One only had so many hours in a day, and the thought of wasting eight of them on one's back—with visions of sugar plumbs and their neurotic dancing—was something a great many people her age weren't up for. Sleep was a good thing in her thirties and forties. Back then, she could use the rest. Now, knowing full well that her time was slipping away, she wanted to get up and use as much of the day as she could.

She got out of bed slowly, her bones aching, her mind jumbled, and she stared out the window. The sun peeked through the clouds, its rays barely making it to her. The sky was one thing that never tired her. She looked up at it, sometimes for hours on end. The blues and the grays of it fascinated her. Sure, her grandchildren found it odd and saw her unending gaze as an excuse to raise a ruckus, but she found peace in the sky. Looking up to the heavens was a special something for her. When the sun slid through the gloom of the clouds, she felt as if she were in the presence of God.

When looking up at the sky as she did each morning, and feeling the sun's warmth on her face, feeling the Almighty right next to her, she often found herself smiling, something she didn't do much elsewhere. Christ was on earth again, and now all those who'd never shared in her age-old optimism had been shown the light. Of course, she'd changed a bit as well with the second coming, never having been one to trust science. She'd doubted them all the way till that fateful Christmas morning when they delivered, both figuratively and literally. Cloning sheep had been one thing, but cloning the Shepherd? She didn't believe it till she saw it with her own eyes on the big screen in Times Square, till she saw the chosen woman holding the baby in her arms. She'd trusted science since that day, as odd as the whole proposition seemed.

Nobody had ever seen the child, except on television, and that plagued her a bit. Plenty of times on screens big and small he'd appeared to let them know he was there and that was good enough for most. He'd become the much more visible God a generation weaned on the boob tube needed, but she didn't understand that need. She didn't understand, "seeing is believing." She'd grown up with nothing more than a radio after all.

She sipped from a glass of orange juice she'd poured the night before and left in the Frigidaire. Her bladder felt heavy after only a few sips and it was off to the bathroom.

The knocking came while she was on the toilet and she moved as fast as she could to wipe her bottom and pull her underpants back on. In her nightie she crept towards the front door, through her darkened apartment, regretting she'd drawn the shades so tightly in the living room. The knocking grew louder and she could feel the vibrations of the door as it was pounded upon, reverberating through the hard wood floor.

Emily peeked through the peephole, careful not to get her

face to close to the banging door. She had no desire for a black eye. It was Samuel, from the third floor. Beyond him and his fist rapping at her door, she could make out tenants running back and forth and a general sense of panic.

As she unlatched the lock, she wondered if she'd missed the fire alarm again. Damn her ears if she had. Maybe a hearing aid was in order.

The banging stopped as she pulled the door open and Samuel came bursting in, ranting and raving for near a minute before Emily finally caught a coherent word.

"You've got to go, Mrs. H. Something bad has happened and you have to get out of the city now."

"What? What's happened?"

Samuel ran about the apartment, grabbing Emily's purse and packing essentials into it: a bottle of water from the fridge, a change of clothing. He stumbled over the furniture as he dashed about.

"Do I have time to get dressed?"

"No, Mrs. H. You have to get out of here now. It's coming right this way."

Emily grabbed hold of Samuel's arm on his next pass through the living room. "What is going on, Samuel?"

"You haven't heard the news?"

"I woke up five minutes ago. What's happened?"

Samuel looked her dead in the eye. "Maybe you should sit down for this."

"I'm not a little girl, Samuel. I'm an old woman and I think I can take whatever you have to tell me."

"You know the Lord's plan to rid the world of sin?"

"I partake in the confessional. Everyone does. I even had the machine installed here to make it easier for myself." Emily motioned towards the awkward looking medical device that hung on her wall beside her phone, a metal box with a cross on it.

Connected to it were two tubes: one ran down into the floor of the apartment, the other hung loose and ended in a needle.

"That machine is the problem, Mrs. H. When people have the sin extracted from their bodies, it has to go somewhere right? All of the sin—I feel so stupid saying that—all of the *chemicals* you're taking out of your body, they have to go somewhere. They go to a plant on the outskirts of the city. They store it all there in huge tanks. Well, there's been an explosion at the facility."

"What does that mean Samuel?"

"Bad things, Mrs. H. Bad things. Some kind of creature has risen out of the spilled chemicals. It's killing everyone that comes within fifty feet of it. If you confess, you're dead. Your body can't handle the pure evil of the thing, and your heart just stops."

"This isn't a joke?"

"No. That's why everyone's trying to get out of here."

Emily followed him out as he tugged on her hand. Her eyes shrank at the light as they stepped down the granite staircase to the street. From one side to the other, she looked. The crowds were moving to the left, and cars packed the street to the right, most of them abandoned. When she squinted down the length of the street she could make out a small bit of the carnage in the distance.

"How are they going to stop it, Samuel?"

"They need people who don't confess."

"You don't mean atheists?" She bit her tongue at the taste of that word rolling across it.

"Yes, atheists."

"Are there any left?"

"Mrs. H., you've got to get going. Head that way. Follow the crowds."

"You aren't coming with me?"

"They need me."

Emily crushed Samuel's wrist in her hand.

"Ow!" he said. "Mrs. H., let go."

"Not you, Samuel. Not you."

"Extraction was never made law, so I never did it."

Emily pulled her brows together and her jaw hurt as she gritted her false teeth. "I don't understand this. You have always been a good, upstanding—"

Samuel wrenched his hand away from her, and he spoke as he rubbed his wrist: "I didn't do anything wrong. Unless of course thinking for myself is wrong. Is it? Are you trying to tell me because I don't bow down before some scientific monstrosity that I'm an awful person?"

"I have no patience for your blaspheming."

"I was an atheist before the asshole in the tower was born, and just because some geneticist picked a speck of blood off the Shroud of Turin and pulled a *Jurassic Park* on it, doesn't mean I'm suddenly going to believe in a higher being. It certainly isn't going to convince me that sticking a needle in my neck every Sunday is going to get me closer to that higher being, regardless."

"I'm going to go," Emily told him, scurrying towards the crowds.

"Good! That's what I wanted you to do in the first place."

She stopped, turned, and stepped back to him. "Why is there such hate in you for the Lord?"

"Mrs. Henderson, God is a bunch of rubbish concocted by some very frightened men a long time ago to explain that which they didn't understand. In my estimation, there's no proof that God exists. And if he did, I still wouldn't worship him. What kind of God leaves his children to rot on a planet like this? What kind of God punishes people like you Mrs. Henderson, who devote the better portion of their lives to him, praising him and spreading his word?"

Emily felt her face grow hot. Her eyes trickled and salty streams crossed her lips. "I thought you a good man, Samuel, but you stand here, full of anger at your creator, at the one who gave you life—"

"My parents gave me life, not some invisible, omnipotent being."

"Why do you need to see things to believe in them?"

"That's the way it is. We live in a scientific world, and if I'm going to believe in God then I want scientific proof."

"The Lord come again on this Earth is not proof enough?"

The sound of the beast grew closer, louder. It was too awesome to ignore now. People were dying and death brought a different kind of scream, one that made Emily's stomach turn. It had been years since she'd heard that scream, since Ernest had gone.

"You've got to go," Samuel told her.

Emily didn't have to squint to see it now. The creature was within sight. Massive it was—at least seven, maybe eight feet tall. Her bottom lip shuddered. It looked like a man but its skin was darker than the most dimly lit closet corner. There was no face to speak of. Its arms were thick and muscled; overall, it looked like something out of one of her grandson's comic books.

"Where is the Lord? Why doesn't he come?" she said.

"He's not coming. He's sitting up in his palace with a bowl of popcorn."

"That is unnecessary."

"So is you still standing here."

"How will you stop it?"

"That group of men and women over there." He motioned towards the solitary throng of unmoving spectators. "We're all…" he said, then paused, looking at his feet. "We're hoping that, since we've never rid ourselves of the chemical, we won't be affected by it."

"What if—?"

A tap on Emily's shoulder came then. Another tenant, the aging British scholar from 304, stood behind her. She couldn't remember his name.

Samuel addressed him. "Nigel, can you get her out of here?"

"Aren't you going?" Nigel asked.

"No."

"Oh." Nigel turned his eyes from Samuel. "Come, Emily," Nigel pressed, his hand on her shoulder.

⚜

THEY RAN FOR FIFTY YARDS. Rather, he ran, and she walked as fast as she could behind him, casting an innumerable number of glances over her shoulder. When she felt far enough away, she stopped. Nigel kept running but Emily stood there, squinting, trying to make out what was happening.

The creature looked like nothing she had ever seen, but its actions were all too familiar to her. She had lived long enough, was probably one of the few left who had, to remember the really bad times, when war was rampant, even commonplace. The carnage it left in its wake reminded her of the second Great War in particular. The bodies and the buildings and the abandoned cars, they reminded her of the newsreels sent home from Europe. But it wasn't in Europe anymore. It was right here.

Emily could see Samuel and she saw him lunge at the beast. He threw a hard right at its face; much to her surprise, the creature not only budged, but buckled as well, collapsing backwards and crushing the overturned car it had been standing on.

"It couldn't have been that easy," she whispered to herself.

As Samuel panted and leaned against a telephone pole the creature snapped back up and threw a fist at him. He was airborne, flying back, back, back until he landed not ten feet from Emily herself. She scampered to him and knelt over his body.

"What are you still...?" Samuel coughed, blood spilling over his lips and dribbling down his chin. "What are you still doing here?"

"This is senseless, Samuel. Come. Run with the rest of us. Save yourself."

Samuel pushed himself up off of the ground and he stumbled a few feet forward. A piece of his rib was jutting through his side. He was soaked in crimson and dripping with perspiration. "The rest... they must've confessed at least once... they... they're all dead."

"And what makes you think you can stop it when they could not?"

"I'm the only one left."

Samuel ran from her, back towards the monstrosity. A trail of red followed him as he leapt onto the hood of a nearby car and then skipped from roof to roof until he was at the feet of the beast again. With what must have been the last bit of strength in him, he leaped towards the creature. This time, something quite different happened.

Emily watched as Samuel was sucked into the abyss of the demon's body. Sparks of yellow burst forth from it, and then streams of whitish blue; the streams of light reached out and grabbed hold of utility poles and any metal they could find. The blue and the yellow combined and the creature was overtaken by an aura the color of a lush springtime garden. It let out a scream that shattered windows—and several-thousand eardrums—and then, then it was gone. Samuel's body dropped onto the hood of the car they had fought on.

BEFORE THE POLICE CAME, Emily stood over the withering corpse. She hunched down and closed his eyes. Looking out over the mess, she wondered what paradise would meet this fate next. But mostly, mostly she pondered the fate of dear Samuel.

Perhaps he was right. Perhaps there was no God. But if there was no God, that meant no heaven, no afterlife, no... She shook her head, clamped her eyelids shut and bit down on her lower lip. "He has to have gone some place," she said. "How will he be repaid? How can I ever repay him?"

They had brought forth the new Christ from a speck of blood on an ancient piece of cloth. Science had triumphed, done what the Church had never been able to do. It had united them all by bringing back their Lord and Savior. It had always seemed like such a victory to her, but now that victory felt hollow, like the empty pit of her stomach.

Perhaps they could clone Samuel. Someone would have to pay for it, but when they knew what he had done, that wouldn't be an issue.

"But you can't clone a soul," she said to herself. "A body, but not a soul."

EMILY STARED out her window at the sun, her eyes locked on it as it sank behind the city's skyline. She had watched the news and they had dealt with it in the same way they had dealt with every other little incident that had risen up in the Lord's second time on Earth. They told the people how sad it was, and how measures were being taken to make sure it never happened again. And then they went directly into the sports segment of the broadcast, as if all of this were nothing more than a glorified car accident, a ten-car pileup at the very most.

Emily didn't eat that night as the calls came in from her family, all of whom were safe, either in the outer boroughs or Upstate. She had time to eat, at least to cook herself a couple of toasted cheese sandwiches, but she couldn't bring herself to do so. The loaf of bread sat on the countertop with two individually wrapped Kraft American singles. While she was on the phone, she glanced over at the untouched food every few minutes. Her stomach growled its opinion. She shook her head, turned her eyes in another direction, and continued her conversations.

WHEN IT WAS time for bed, Emily didn't even need to change. She was still in her nightie. She hadn't bothered to get dressed, hadn't seen the point. From her nightstand, she grabbed a picture of Ernest, her dear husband, twenty years gone. She wrapped her arms around it and slipped under the covers, praying this would be the night. She prayed for a reunion.

Emily thought about him all the time, but not since those days immediately following his passing had she prayed to be taken, to taken to him. She had relearned life, had found a way to keep going in the faces of her children and grandchildren, but they couldn't help her with this latest dilemma. She had listened to their words coming through the telephone, had tried to smile when they asked her to, but none of it helped. She needed her Ernest now. She had been strong for twenty years without him, but this latest bit—she could not bear alone. She wanted Ernest to hold her in his arms. She wanted to smell him, that scent that wafted into the house before he did, the smell of grease and the garage. And when she'd kissed his lips again, like she had on the docks in Hyannis that first time, on one of her vacations to Cape Cod, she would find the other man she needed to find. She would find Samuel and tell him she was sorry.

Emily closed her eyes, hoping they would not open again on this horrible world.

❧

EMILY GOT out of bed at eight A.M. By then she'd fallen in and out of sleep at least six times, and experienced quite a few strange dreams. The smell that filled her apartment was not the smell of grease and the garage. Instead, it was the smell of freshly fallen rain. Emily stepped over to her window, careful to avoid the piles of shattered glass. From behind a cloud, the sun peeked out at her.

As the sun slid through the gloom, she was surprised that He was still there. She had expected Him to go. He didn't break bread with those who wished for their own demise, did He?

"Not my time?" she asked the sky.

There was no response.

"A common man, an atheist—someone who doesn't even believe in You—he saved us. Not your *son*. But is that even your son?"

The clouds shrank away. Just the weather? Or something more?

"He's not, is he? We can clone a body, but not a spirit."

The sky was at once clear and bright, deep cerulean blue. She looked about for the clouds, but they had completely gone. They could not have disappeared so fast, could they?

"There will be no second coming, no return."

The sun's heat grew fiercer, more intense. She could feel the sweat beading up under her arms, and behind her knees.

"Man must figure it out for himself."

Emily looked down to the street. Crowds were gathering. She wasn't the only one to see all this.

"Man doesn't need the hand of God to solve his problems."

Emily smiled, perspiration pouring over her face.

"You have faith in us." She beamed. "You have faith in us."

Emily Henderson stepped back from the window and headed towards the shower.

EZEKIEL AND THE HARVESTERS

"**A**n Amish rock band?" Nigel questioned, adjusting his spectacles.

"Yeah, they're fucking amazing. Best shit I've heard since the Fab Four themselves."

"Didn't quite peg you for a Beatles fan, Ben."

"Well you don't know me that well." Ben opened the jewel-case and then snapped it shut. "So, you wanna hear it or what?"

"How did you get a recording of an Amish band? They're deathly afraid of recording devices, aren't they?"

"You've been out of the loop for a while haven't you Nigel. It's called a bootleg. Somebody snuck into one of their shows and recorded it."

"I'm quite aware of what a bootleg is, Ben. I'm forty-nine, not dead." Nigel scratched the skin behind his left ear. "I just don't understand why someone would violate the religious beliefs of a group of people like that for a quick buck. I simply cannot comprehend it."

"Well it's their religion that got them into this. If their religion allowed metal detectors, the tape recorder might never have gotten into the show to begin with. You're such a goody two shoes, Nigel. They're a great fucking band, and their religion shouldn't stand in the way of their success. This CD'll prove it to you. Here," he said, offering the disc to him, "Have a listen."

"I'd rather not. If I'm going to hear this band, it'll be under their terms."

"You're gonna drive all the way to fuckin' Pennsylvania?"

"Maybe. I do have some vacation time coming up."

"What-fuckin-ever man. Whatever floats your boat. You should just listen to the CD, and save yourself the gas money. I'll see ya later. I'm gonna go give this thing another listen."

"Good night," Nigel replied, turning back to the stairs and resuming his climb.

Nigel smiled as he passed by the venerable old landlady on his way up. "How are you tonight, Emily?"

"Just fine Nigel. Say, have you heard anything of this group Benjamin is blaring on his stereo? It seems to me they're all the rage these days. What were they called again?"

"Ezekiel and the Harvesters, I think."

"Yes, that's it," she proclaimed, smiling, "Quite a shame they can't make recordings of themselves. They'd make a pretty penny, I'd bet. It's a silly religion they practice, those Amish folks."

Nigel smiled, ascending the stairs to the third floor, where his own apartment lay. "Quite a silly religion indeed."

"Yes, good night, Nigel."

Excerpt from the journal of Nigel Mackman
October 5, 1994

The curiosity is killing me. I so wanted to listen to that CD tonight. I've been hearing about Ezekiel and the Harvesters for weeks now, and how they are next Beatles, the next big thing. The whole world is sick of this grunge music, sick of twenty-somethings whining about problems we're all already well aware of. The people want something poppy, something light to take their minds off of things, and they are all saying this band is it; this band is the answer. I so wanted to listen to that CD.

That CD! I just heard on the news that the band is about to break up because of it. They say that they cannot continue with this project for fear of further violating their religious beliefs. They're going to do one last concert and that'll be all. Great. Bloody great. My only chance to see them, and the whole damned world is sure to be there. It'll be in one week, just outside of Hershey, Pennsylvania.

I have to see them. Lord knows how much I regret having missed the first Fab Four all those years ago. If only I hadn't been so snooty, I could've been there the moment it was birthed into the world, the first meeting of Lennon and McCartney at the Woolton Village Fete, but I was the snobbish piano prodigy, too good for lowly skiffle music.

Oh bother! How many times am I going to relive that bloody story, and waste even more of this paper? I'm not going to miss my chance to be part of something that special again. I'm going to Pennsylvania!

⊙⚙۶

NIGEL WOKE EARLY the next morning, called in sick to work, and began to pack. His boss wasn't happy with him. Who was to cover his classes? Professor Patterson would just have to make due. The only thing that mattered to Nigel was getting to Pennsylvania for the concert.

He packed only the essentials: clothes, bathroom supplies, and his Beatles audiotape collection to listen to in the car on the way. He gave Ben a ring to see if maybe he wanted to hitch a ride, but he was nowhere to be found. There would be no traveling companion this time out. *All the better*, he supposed. He wasn't sure a week's worth of Ben's vulgarity was what he had in mind.

Nigel showered fast then threw his things into his '87 Ford Tempo, a bothersome gray money-pit of a car, the only vehicle his measly salary could afford. He climbed into the car and he was off.

It would be a long ride from Los Angeles to Amish County, Pennsylvania, probably a week's worth of travel at the pace he'd planned. He'd get there just in time.

Around noon that day he crossed the California border. He stopped for a Quarter Pounder with Cheese at McDonalds and continued on. Nigel wanted to be in Phoenix by dark and it was an attainable goal. Traffic wasn't that bad, and he was cruising at a steady 65. People were passing him. He smiled and sang harmony with his radio just the same.

He made it to Phoenix around nine o'clock, stopping at a diner in the suburbs for dinner. The waitress brought him his simple meal, (a French dip, fries, and a Coke,) with a genuine disinterest. He ate it quickly and left her a five percent tip, modest by most standards, but generous in his eyes, considering her service.

The night brought what would be the first of many cheap hotel rooms. He did, after all, have to make this trip as cost-effective as possible. His savings account left very little margin for error.

With his sweat-stained shirt peeled off, he lay on the bed, wondering if every day would be this tiring. Tiring. He was pathetic. Twenty years ago he would've been half way there by now. Now, as much as he tried to deny it, his muscles ached, and his hair seemed to gray more with each passing breath.

He sighed, rolled over and reached for the TV clicker. No cable, just local channels. News. *Click*. Weather. *Click*. Game show. *Click*. Nothing.

"Bloody hell. Might as well just get to sleep." He reached for the pillow behind him, fluffed it up, and lay his head down.

THE NEXT TWO days were just as uneventful as the first. He drove, ate, and slept. He showered too, and stopped to wash up at just about every gas station he passed, the grit and grime of the road seeping into every pore of him. He'd made it half way across the country, mostly out of a lack of things to do. He didn't stop to see sights, only spent enough time to rest up for the next part of the journey.

The things he did notice weren't pleasant. Cold commercialism consumed every street corner. Vendors peddled their meaningless garbage everywhere at obscene prices. Men and women slept under bridges and on park benches, while the others, the fortunate ones, carried heaps of overstuffed plastic bags bearing the likeness of a cartoon mouse, all for their spoiled children. Give them stuff, and stuff, and more stuff, so that they never end up under a bridge. Stuff was the savior of mankind.

He only deviated from his course when absolutely necessary.

The third day ended on a down note. He blew out a tire somewhere around Oklahoma City. A tow truck found him on the highway and told him it'd take just a day to fix. He checked into another mediocre motel, pulled out his journal, and began to write.

෴

Excerpt from the journal of Nigel Mackman
October 8, 1994

DEPRESSION, *I've been told, is a common occurrence when engaged in road trips by one's self. I didn't actually believe it until today. I don't have many acquaintances at home, but even the total strangers that sit beside me on the daily bus ride are better than eight hours accompanied by only an empty seat.*

I am seriously beginning to wonder if I'll make it to Pennsylvania, whether I'll ever get to see The Harvesters. Is it even worth my trouble?

I haven't been this downtrodden in quite a while. Half of it is the bloody car, but the other half, I think, is just doubts. Am I too old for this?

Am I stupid for traveling across the country to see a band I've never even heard? People my age are relegated to the symphony, Barry Manilow, and, when we're feeling really dangerous, the Stones.

What does "on their terms" mean anyway?

I'm really tired, and I think I should just go to bed.

IT TOOK Nigel quite a while to get up that next morning. He'd not even stirred when the light came pouring into his window at eleven. When he did stir, he saw his alarm flash 12:00, absolutely useless thanks to a power outage. He had slept in and given the delays he'd already suffered that was not good.

He showered quickly, not doing much more than scrubbing the grit out of his hair. Paying his bill at the main desk, he noticed how much lighter his wallet had become. The clerk gave him a message from the auto mechanic: the car was fixed and he was all set. Nigel hitched a ride with the motel owner's son. The son doled out a smile that kept him to his side of the truck's bench seat. It was the longest ride around the block he'd ever experienced, but he reached the mechanic unscarred. He was on his way by three o'clock.

His collection of Beatles tapes rode shotgun, a heap of magnetic tape and gray plastic. He'd listened to them over and over during the course of the trip and in between tapes he would listen to the local radio stations fading in and out, sometimes sliding inaudibly beneath the static. All of them detailed the latest breaking developments in the Harvesters' saga, and though most of them were abiding by the band's request to not play the bootleg on the air, every once in a while a station would break the ban and throw it on. No more than a few seconds into it, Nigel would either have another tape popped in, or the channel changed.

If I'm going to hear this group, it'll be under their terms.

Still, the few times he hadn't changed the channel or popped in the tape fast enough, he had managed to catch a second or two of the opening licks to the song. And just that second or two was enough to bait him. Each time that hook was a little bit harder to avoid.

Somewhere around the Ohio/Pennsylvania border, a day later, Nigel grew tired of Liverpudlian love songs. He scanned the radio stations, looking for something new, something fresh to keep him awake. It had been dark for an hour and a half by now, and his heavy eyes informed him he must stop for the night somewhere soon and continue his journey the next morning. Each time he blinked, it was a bit harder to un-blink, to pry those lids open again.

"And now, lets give a listen to the latest, and greatest thing to hit the airwaves," said the announcer with his thick baritone.

Nigel stole his ring finger from the scan button and the DJ continued, "...here's Ezekiel and the Harvesters with 'Field Hand' on Pennsylvania's Number One, 92.5..."

He should've turned it off right away, but he didn't. He couldn't. That opening riff was transcribed onto his skull and it was painful: one page of the music there clear as day in his mind, the next page unable to be flipped to. He couldn't bear to hear it and change the station again.

The song started with the catchy twang of an acoustic guitar: B flat strummed six times, then D in the same manner, and finally an E flat, then over again; a simple melody, but it was catchy. The second guitar chimed in after four measures, picking out notes here and there, in a style unthinkable for all but the most talented classical or flamenco player. The string bass recalled visions of Elvis and a hound dog. The drums reminded him of Charlie Watts and his simple, disinterested backbeat.

Then came that voice. The singer was a tenor with a wide range, and no fear of the high notes. He sang of working in the field and the temptations of the world, and how he overcame them on a daily basis to retain his place in the Amish community.

Amish. It was so hard to believe that these people, with their outdated value system could produce such wonderful music. He was entranced, uplifted, and had almost forgotten how tired he was.

Three and a half minutes later it was over, and he was in love.

Excerpt from the journal of Nigel Mackman
Early October 10, 1994

CHECKED *into a hotel about a half-hour away from the concert site at about 12:15 A.M. The traffic coming out of Hershey was horrendous. There was a big Antique Car show this past week, and everybody is going home. That bloody song was stuck in my head the whole time, and it took quite a while for its spell to wear off, for the sleepiness to return. I really cannot fathom the way it sounded, not just the band itself, but the recording. It was a far clearer reproduction than any other bootleg I've ever encountered.*

Ah, what a wonderful night. I have found something to latch on to, so to speak. My fiftieth birthday is coming up and I was beginning to feel it was time to start digging my grave. I don't know. I felt so tired until tonight, but that song—that wonderful, wonderful song!—it has given me hope, and strength. Maybe I did miss the chance to see the world's greatest band those many years ago, but I have a feeling that this time it's going to be different. I'm going to experience Ezekiel and the Harvesters. I am. I am!

NIGEL WOKE and hopped into the shower of the third-rate hotel, praying for hot water. What he got was a trickle, then a slow-moving stream of lukewarm liquid. He wasn't sure it was water. He wasn't sure what it was. It had a sort of yellowish tint, but it was close enough to water that he didn't care. The blast of cold air that waited on the other side of the shower curtain stunned him and for a moment he forgot what was next.

Nigel shaved, relieved himself in the barely functioning toilet, and dried himself off with a towel made Swiss cheese by cigarette burns. The conditions were horrible but it didn't bother him. Today was the day, his chance to be part of rock and roll history, his second chance. And he wasn't going to blow this one.

His clothes were picked carefully. There was no need to encourage the younger fans to persecute him. He chose his one pair of blue jeans, a plain white T-shirt and a flannel, not as much to fit in with the so-called "grungers" as to keep warm on the chilly October afternoon. He combed his thinning hair back from his brow, and put on his "coolest" pair of glasses, as he did before every concert he'd been to these past few years.

He wasn't fond of music these days, but the American music scene was one of the few places a nearly fifty-something could go to feel young again. Perhaps that's why he'd taken to the Harvesters so fast. It was the knowledge that no longer would he have to settle for mediocre music in his hopeless quest for the fountain of youth. Now he'd have some really good music to listen to as nature wiped her hands of him. Some really good music.

In his car that afternoon, he wondered what the stage would look like. He wondered where they could possibly fit as many people as were likely to show up and still have the music be loud enough. There would be no amps, no P.A., just the acoustics of the venue. No light show would be in store. How would they do it? There would be no electricity period.

At least not the real kind. There will most certainly be some manner of "electricity" between the performers and their audience.

Fifteen minutes down the road came the first signs, reading

things like: "This way to Ezekiel!" and, "The Harvesters' Last Concert, LIVE in Intercourse, PA!"

Americans chuckled over this vulgarly named town in the heart of Amish county, but the locals weren't referring to sexual practices when they christened their community. They were referring to the major intersection, or intercourse of roads.

Silly, perverted, America.

Growing more excited by the moment, he turned on the radio.

"This is Al Williams reporting live from the site of Ezekiel and the Harvesters farewell concert. The crowds are arriving. The concession stands are here. Everyone is gearing up for what is sure to be the show of the century."

Nigel smirked. *And I'm going to be there. I am going to be there.*

"I've just spoken with Ezekiel, Zachariah, Abraham, and Jonah, off tape of course, and to say that they are going through a maelstrom of emotions right now would be an understatement of gargantuan proportions. And who can blame them? This band, which has skyrocketed to the upper echelon of the American music scene in the past two months, is now being forced to leave behind a prosperous career because of the greed of one man, one man who needed to have them on tape. As it happened with McCartney's proclamation all those years ago, this act, like the original Fab Four, is ending years before its time. Whoever you are, shame on you! And now, to get you all excited here is that song, from that bootleg, it's Ezekiel and the Harvesters, with 'Field Hand'."

Bloody imbeciles! They fucked it up for all of us, dammit! Nigel slammed his fist into the dashboard in frustration and then something he'd never expected to happen happened. He'd never expected it, but he should have.

My bloody car stalled. MY BLOODY FUCKING CAR STALLED!!! He pulled it to the side of the road, got out, and opened the hood. Steam billowed from the engine. "Bloody hell," he whispered to himself. "BLOODY HELL!"

"Can I help you, sir?" a voice asked from behind him as the traffic whizzed by.

"Not unless your an automobile mechanic," he said, kicking his bumper before spinning around. There before him, dressed all up in a suit and cloak the color of midnight, was an Amish gentleman, just descended from his buggy.

"A mechanic'll do you no good sir. These things are unreliable monstrosities."

"Not all cars are unreli—"

"It's a Ford. Fix Or Repair Daily, I believe, is the expression." He tapped the hood of the Tempo, and smirked. "That buggy back there," he pointed," has been in my family for three generations. Now that's a reliable vehicle."

"Look, I don't need to be preached to, Mister... Mister... I'm sorry I didn't get your name."

"Not important that you know it, for I'll be departing shortly, just as soon as I help you on your way."

"Sir, I need a ride to the Ezekiel and the Harvesters concert."

The Amishman shook his head and ran his fingers through his graying beard. "Ezekiel and the Harvesters. Is that right? I should have figured as much. You dimwits *are* all the same."

"Dimwits? What's crawled up your ass? Are you telling me you don't like their music? I... I... Surely, even if you don't like their music you must take comfort in their stellar representation of your people and your culture to the world."

The Amishman peered under the hood of the car. He squinted his eyes at something and came up looking puzzled. He sighed, "Their music is not what's important. It's that they've violated our principles. That's what bothers me."

"But they didn't make the bootleg. Some greedy capitalist bastard did."

"That's not what I'm talking about, sir. You don't know, do

you? None of you know. Is there even an ounce of common sense left in this world?"

"Well if this is some sort of Amish secret, how can you expect us to? You don't bloody communicate with the rest of the us."

"Perhaps that's because we find it difficult to deal with the way the rest of the world conducts itself."

"If you're not going to talk to us, how can you expect us to know what it is that you don't like about your kinsman? Aren't you supposed to be peaceful and supportive of your brother? Whatever happened to that?"

"They are not my brothers!" the Amishman screamed, his face flush with anger. "They are a gaggle of musicians from Los Angeles that one of your record companies put together and called Amish. They are a marketing ploy. You find a bunch of near-talented folks, give them a handicap, and the world loves them. My religion is no handicap!" The Amishman paused, breathed deep once and then again. Finally, he asked, "Do you need help or don't you, sir?'

Nigel rubbed his eyes, pinched the bridge of his nose, and took a second to peer down at the ground.

"Do you need help, sir?" the Amishman asked again, this time a bit more calm.

"No," he began, his face pale, his mind numb, "I've a cell phone in my car. I'll call a tow truck."

"Then, good day," the Amishman said, tipping his hat then turning away, "And please, pay no heed to my outburst. My only wish is that we could expose these men." He stepped up into his buggy. "Alas, your so-called rumor mill has already made them the stuff of legend. And who's going to believe a man stuck in the dark ages over one of your respected record executives anyway?"

Nigel stood speechless as the Amishman rode away. *Why would anyone...?* He wondered.

He turned back to his car, thought of his job, and the relatively cushy life he was leading. *Everyone wants to be lazy.* He looked again to the buggy as it faded off behind a cluster of trees. *Except them.*

Nigel got into his car, and turned the key. It purred to life as if nothing had ever happened. He could still make it to the concert. He still had a chance to see the new Fab Four. *Under their terms.*

Nigel put on his blinker, cut his way through the traffic, took his first left, not caring where it would lead him, and threw caution to the wind.

HACKER

"FUCK 'EM!" he screamed, throwing his withering '85 Escort into park, turning it off and yanking the key from the ignition in one fluid movement. He slammed his fist into the dashboard. "Fuck them and their stupid rules."

Ben stomped up the front steps of the apartment building, and pulled the door open. Mrs. Henderson, the sweet, silver-haired landlady was at the next door, and as she unlocked it he rushed through with flagrant disregard for her.

"FUCK!" he screamed as he rammed his key into the hole, and pushed his way into his apartment. He threw his apron to the side into a pile of unwashed laundry and trampled through the mess of his home, nearly crushing the cat that lay harmless on the floor. "Fucking thing," he screamed, raising his foot to kick it. "Yeah, that's right. Run the fuck away."

He made it to his bedroom and flicked on the light, sitting down at his decrepit, disease-ridden Mac and pushing the mouse around until the screen flickered its various shades of gray. 'I'm not dead yet,' it proclaimed with an obnoxious ping. He pushed the mouse over to Fuckface, the appropriately named hard drive, and double-clicked. The folder opened, he scrolled down to AOL, and again he double-clicked. With his free hand, he pulled solitary strands of greasy brown hair out by the roots. He waited patiently for the connection to be made, and for the annoying little voice to tell him he had mail. The cat wandered in from the other room. "What the fuck do you want?" he asked it.

The cat said nothing, staring back at him with every ounce of feline indifference in its body.

Ben turned back to the screen and saw the main page, and of course, he had no mail. It was typical. Nobody ever wrote him. "Look pussy, nobody loves me. Isn't that a shame?" He screamed and threw his *Internet for Dummies* book at the unsuspecting cat, nailing it square in the head. It squealed and ran away. Ben laughed, then said, "That's the fucking funniest thing I've seen all day."

Ben went through the drawn out process of checking his daily sites: WWF.com, NewsAskew, and Cinescape. It seemed to take even longer on this piece of crap. He'd been so much happier with his PC, but after its little 'accident' last week, this second-hand, five-year-old Macintosh was the only thing a lowly cashier at Wal-Mart could manage. This was all his shitty job could afford, and now he didn't even have the shitty job. All he had was his computer, his only friend in the world.

"Benjamin," called Mrs. Henderson from the other room. "Benjamin, are you all right? You were in quite a rush just now, and it seemed as though something was wrong. Benjamin, is there something I can do?"

"Yeah," he bellowed, "close the fucking door."

The door snapped shut. Little old lady had no patience for vulgarity in her home. Fuck her and her principles.

Ben returned to his computing. It didn't take long to discover there was no new news and no new entries on any of the Web journals he followed. Nothing. Now where would he go? *Ah yes*, he thought to himself. He moved his mouse to the location bar, and began to type: www.playboy.com.

It took him a few minutes but he finally found his way to the previously unpublished pictures section, his favorite. Unpublished or not, it didn't really matter. He'd never managed to find the money—or the gall—to go out and buy an issue anyway. He dreamed of the things he would do to these girls, and he could feel the excitement building in his pants, but he knew he'd never have them. They were all off in Beverly Hills somewhere, fucking over the hill rock stars. That's what they all did. All of them. Models and rock stars. It made him sick. Why didn't they want to be with him?

He gave himself a once over. *That's why, idiot.*

"I have to find a real woman," he muttered to himself, getting up and walking to the kitchen. "I'm sick of looking and not being able to touch." From the fridge, he grabbed himself a Rolling Rock. "Can't afford a whore. Can't exactly call Samantha. Bitch went to town on my heart with a meat tenderizer after dragging me all the way from L.A. to Beantown." He maneuvered through half-empty pizza boxes and heaps of two-week-old laundry until the answer came to him on the pages of the *Internet for Dummies* book, which lay half open, stained on one corner by a spot of the bad kitty's blood. "A chat room!" He wailed jubilantly, "I'll find a real woman in a chat room. There's got to be at least a few, and we won't go to just any room."

He ran back into the bedroom and leapt across his raggedy twin bed, its covers balled up on one end. "We'll make a visit to L'Hotel. Haven't been there in a few weeks." All he got from typing "lhotel.com" was an error message telling him that the URL couldn't be found. The address wasn't that simple, he remembered. Tossing papers left and right, he searched for the address until all the papers that had been on his desk littered the floor with all the other refuse. "SHIT!" He screamed again, "Where the fuck is it?"

For a man who vehemently despised the inadequacies of search engines, there was only one viable alternative. He didn't enjoy using his talent, but that was all he had. It wasn't that he didn't find it useful. He did. The problems were the headaches and the nosebleeds. The harder he pushed, the more grotesque the side effects were. He was determined though, as was his cock, to get laid.

He had to find a woman tonight. Only catch was, it had to be a woman with some bank to pay for a hotel room. He certainly wasn't going to score in the midst of this pigsty.

I'm twenty-three years old and I've never been touched by a woman anywhere below the equator. Samantha and her principles. My love wasn't strong enough to drop her drawers?

He laid his hand carefully on the mouse, barely touching it. His *talent* necessitated delicacy, so he couldn't manhandle the equipment in his usual manner. Ben closed his eyes and concentrated. A disturbing blue obliterated the blackness. Hundreds of millions of zeroes and ones mixed with line upon line of more decipherable code: HTML, CSS, and JavaScript. He felt his head quake as the information super-highway flooded before his eyes. The rush of information was like a shot of heroin. It fucked with his mind at first, but eventually provided clarity unreachable by any other means. Code flew by at ungodly speeds, CSS cutting off JavaScript in a play for control of the fast lane, while HTML did a humble 55 ignoring the honks of the flashier, more Porsche-like code riding its ass. He tried to conjure the words 'L' Hotel Chat' out of the madness, until finally, through the murk, it rose to the surface. Out of the maelstrom of letters and numbers came the familiar opening page. He opened his eyes and there it was on the screen. He smiled.

His head throbbed uncontrollably, but at least he hadn't gotten a nosebleed. The Lobby menu popped up, giving him the option to check the guest book but Ben didn't feel like it. No one he knew would be around. He typed his name into the box that sat beside the 'Enter the Lobby' button and he hit return, sure he would find his woman here tonight.

The stark white of L' Hotel's double paned Lobby screen popped up and Ben took a quick glance over the messages sliding up in the lower pane. LittlePerv(m13) was posting sex pictures, and pretty graphic ones at that, the kind you only found on sites that warned 'Adults Only. If you are under 18 please click here,' then provided a link to Disney.com to those who clicked. As if kids paid attention to that shit.

"Any ladies out there looking to have a good time tonight IRL?"

Someone typed IRL?!? Fuck! All these bullshit chat abbreviations pissed him off. If someone out there wanted to say 'in real life,' why didn't they just say 'in real life' and not regurgitate 'IRL?' As he scrolled down, looking for any leads, he noticed her.

The message read, "JACKIE *says to Mark:* I would really like to meet you... you sound like you could fulfill my fantasy well." Ben cracked a smile. *Finally, a horny chick.*

The message was followed quickly by another: "JACKIE *says to ALL:* Shit, that was supposed to be private."

Ben's grin was uncontrollable. "She must be pretty hot for this Mark asshole, talking about fantasies and shit. Maybe..." He was giddy.

He held the mouse and closed his eyes. Navigating through line after line of bullshit code, he finally reached Mark's computer.

Ben stared at the Internet address on Mark's screen, the key to sending messages under his name. He stared at it, memorizing each number as the late night traffic surged around him. Mark was trying to type and Ben could feel every keystroke, one after another, beating into his temples. This fucker typed loud. Every key he hit was like a blast to the head with ball-peen hammer. *Take a typing class, you asshole!*

As a parting shot, and as thanks for his now throbbing temples, Ben loosed a virus onto Mark's hard drive.

He opened his eyes and felt the salty taste of blood cross his lips. He had stayed in too long. With a stray piece of paper, he wiped his nose clean. On screen, Jackie was writing drawn out pleas to anyone who could help her find out what happened to Mark. Ben tried not to chuckle.

He typed in the address, hoping the computer wouldn't give him any shit, and it didn't. The white of the screen turned black for a second, then the lobby reappeared and the name on Ben's screen was no longer his own.

Ben typed fast and furious. "Jackie I'm OK... had some computer problems." And this was of course completely believable. Those sort of things happened in this 'room' all the time. He couldn't control his grin.

What had they been talking about? Scrolling through their conversation, he gathered information fast. Jackie was a lonely, but attractive woman in Boston, just about ten minutes across town. She was looking for a man to fulfill her fantasy, which was to make love to a total stranger.

Mark's some guy. I hope the new hard drive doesn't set him back.

They had made plans already when Ben interrupted and took Mark's place. Most promising of all, the physical description Mark gave was vague enough for Ben to pull off. He scrolled back down to find a message from Jackie waiting.

"JACKIE *privately whispers to Mark:* So are we all set?"

Ben smiled and typed. "Mark *privately whispers to JACKIE:* Yeah... I'll see you in an hour."

"JACKIE *privately whispers to Mark:* I'll be waiting"

※

FIFTEEN MINUTES OF SUAVE, Colgate, and Lever 2000 later, Ben was dressing, throwing on the cleanest pair of underwear he could find, one of his pairs of black jeans, and an Aerosmith concert shirt. He combed his hair neatly into place, grabbed his keys, and bolted out the door.

It was a quick drive, much quicker than he had expected, so when he got there he didn't want to go straight in. He circled the block once, surveying the surroundings. It seemed like a boring neighborhood. The second time he circled he noticed someone peek out the window of a first floor apartment. It had to be her. He circled one last time to get a better look. She was tall and thin, with ample breasts and a nice looking coif of red hair. He was ready, and it seemed she was too. She was alternating glances between the street and her watch.

He pulled into the lot and parked the car, then dashed up the stairs and into the building to search the wall for the button that read "JACKIE RHODES." The button found and pressed, he waited, tapping his foot. The buzzer went off and he pulled the door open.

He walked calmly down the hallway. A few feet short of her doorway, he stopped to look himself over in the reflection coming off a fire extinguisher. *Not all that bad.* Sure, he had the beginnings of a beer gut, but Mark did too, and this woman was ready to sleep with him.

He glanced down. His bulge had grown significantly during the trek from the front door. *Not too bad at all.* He was Mark Monahan, the man of Jackie's dreams.

At the doorway he smiled and knocked.

The door opened and revealed his prize. An oversized t-shirt hung on her, accentuating all the right parts. Burgundy hair flowed down to her shoulders and he grew drunk on that hair. Her body curved perilously, driving every ounce of blood in his body to his throbbing crotch. There was barely enough left elsewhere to keep him upright. Just looking at her was enough to burst a cylinder, never mind touching her. He could come just imagining it.

"Who are you?" she asked.

He took her into his arms, holding her close to feel the heat of her body, and he kissed her. With his tongue sliding into her saccharine little mouth and his hands crawling underneath her shirt, he thought he might lose it right there. To kiss her gently was a struggle, but he wanted for her to like him. If it was good the first time, there might be second time, and a third. Besides, Mark was probably gentle.

They kissed and kissed until they were on the floor, their clothes scattered, each of their fantasies coming true.

❁

SEVERAL HOURS LATER, as dawn crept through the blinds of the apartment they woke. She kissed him tenderly on the lips. "It was wonderful, Mark."

He tried not to show his disgust. She was amazing and he never wanted this to end, but he was sick of Mark. She'd been calling out his name all night, and it nauseated him. "My name is not Mark."

"What do you mean, silly?" she said, a flighty schoolgirl grin on her face as she ran her fingers through his hair.

He stopped her. "I am not Mark."

She pulled away from him and sat up, covering herself with the blankets, "Who are you?" Her happy-got-lucky smile degraded into a look of repulsion. "What the fuck is going on here?"

The concern on his face grew. He wanted her to like him. He *needed* her to. This was his only chance. Samantha had scorned him, and other woman offered no more than indifferent glances. This couldn't be happening. Mark was ruining everything. She had to love him. "I...I"

"YOU WHAT?!?" She screamed, "Who the hell are you? What the fuck did you do to Mark?"

Ben shook his head and pulled his hair out of his face. He was sick of this, and he had to make her understand. "I hacked into his system when you two were talking last night, and I took his place. I read all his messages to you, all his talk about fucking, when you wanted to make love. He wasn't right for you, so I figured I would step in."

She got out of bed and pulled on the first shirt she could find. "You figured you'd take his place? You're an asshole! I wanted Mark, not some lowlife piece of shit like you. That hacking stuff is a violation of privacy. You lied to me."

"NO!" He screamed, "You wanted a stranger, and that's what I gave you."

"I... I"

"You said you wanted to fuck a stranger. You really just wanted to role-play. You're out there in the chat room, prancing around like a little slut, telling people you want to 'make love to a stranger.' Well I got news for you. You don't go around the net telling people that and expect not to get taken up on your offer."

"Get out of my house," she demanded, tears racing down her cheeks. "Get out of my house!"

"No. We can work this out. We have to work this out. I'm sure we can get beyond this. I've done you a great favor. I know the kind of scum that lurks out there. I saved you. I'm sure that you can learn to love me, after what I've done for you."

"What?!" She howled, "You think I'm gonna love you? You're nuts. Get the hell out of my house, you fucking psychopath."

He leapt across the bed and pushed her up against the wall. "Listen bitch, you will love me. You will!" He stared her down, the tears still flowing, her freckled cheeks white and wet with fear.

"Don't cry," he said to her, loosening his grip. He was over the top. He had to be calm. "Baby, don't cry. It's unbecoming."

"Fuck you!" she shrieked, jamming her knee into his crotch.

Ben toppled onto the carpet, his eyes watering as she drew closer and closer to the door. She was getting away.

He closed his eyes. He'd never done it from this far away, this quickly, or in this much pain. But she was it: his last chance at everything. The black turned to blue and the number strings that ran the security system flew through his head. He concentrated, only one word coming to his mind. Lock. LOCK. *LOCK.* ***LOCK!***

He opened his eyes and there she was at the door, trying desperately to tear it open. "You... you shouldn't have tried that. I only want for you to love me."

She seized a vase from its shelf and ran towards him. Ben ducked and her momentum sent her flying over him, face first into the thick carpet. He spun around and leapt on top of her.

"Do I have to make you love me?" He ran his fingers through her hair as she lay whimpering below him. He had to make her love him, his succulent princess with her red hair, and her exquisitely carved body. He had to make her love him and so he did. He made her love him right there. She still wouldn't scream his name; she was screaming 'NO!' the whole time. But 'NO,' he supposed, was better than Mark.

❀

With his talent, he spent the next hour reprogramming her home for her protection. He shut off her phone and removed the modem from her computer. Then he hacked the security system and changed the code to something only he would know. The world was too dangerous for Jackie. She didn't need all of those burdens anymore. He would take care of her now. He closed the blinds. The sun would be bad for her in her present condition.

Why hadn't she gotten up yet?

Blood oozed from his nose. His head was throbbing too, but he seemed to be hurting less than before. Jackie was his now and nothing else mattered, not even the pain. He'd made her love him.

Quivering on the floor, her skin was one shade darker than coma white.

"I have to go back to my place to pick up a few things, dear. I'll be back in about an hour. Will you be OK?"

She didn't move.

He glanced around the apartment. It was superbly decorated, he supposed, at least from her point of view. The off-white wall-paper barely showed under all of the paintings and photographs. He guessed she must have loved this place. It was cozy.

He didn't like cozy. When he got back, he would have to do something about all this.

She shuddered for a second and went still again. Her only constant movement was the rising and falling of her chest.

He smiled. She was just resting. Maybe he'd been too much man for her. He'd never been with anyone else, so for all he knew, he was too much man for anyone. "OK," he said unlocking the door, "I'll be back."

On his way out, he tripped on something, a stuffed rabbit with big brown eyes, and droopy ears. It was a shame she had to be so sappy. He tossed it aside.

At the door he turned to say to her, "Goodbye, Honey."

Her lips trembled.

"I love you too, Honey. I'll be back soon."

VAMP

Sarah just wasn't the same. There was something different in her eyes. They didn't seem as deep, as bright. The rest of her seemed normal: her short brown hair, a perfect halo accentuating her face in a way that it was hard not to stare; her body, just as lean and toned as usual. She was dressing a bit more dangerously, a lower cut shirt here and there. Her jeans were a little too tight every once in a while, but she'd done this before, when she was feeling particularly good about herself. She liked to look good. Most people did. Not much had changed, but her eyes —there was something different about her eyes.

She was eating her spaghetti casually, not speaking. Every few minutes she'd flash him a little smile, but that was it. He twirled his spaghetti around his fork. He hadn't had a bite and she hadn't noticed. She always noticed things like that. She was always concerned about whether or not he liked what she had cooked, even something as simple as pasta. She hadn't noticed. It irritated him even more.

"Are you all right?"

She looked up for a second. Smile. "Of course. Why do you ask?"

"No reason."

Done with her meal, she picked up her plate and glass and took them to the sink. He heard the running of water, then the opening and closing of the dishwasher. She returned a few minutes later. "I've got a late appointment. Client couldn't meet any other time."

"OK. When will you be back?"

"Late. It's a double session, and then me and Christina are going out for a drink. I'll see you tomorrow."

He dropped his fork. "All right."

THEY HADN'T SPENT a night together since the fight two weeks ago. That's when the changes seemed to begin. She'd stormed out and slammed the door so loud that it warranted a visit from Mrs. Henderson, the landlady. She was a little nosy, but a nice old woman just the same.

The fight was still fresh in his memory. They'd been in bed. First she wanted him on top of her, hard and fast. Then she wanted nothing more than him caressing her, rubbing her all over. Then she wanted him inside of her again. Then she told him to get off. Nothing was bringing her to her peak.

This time she was more frustrated with herself than him. He always came quickly. It was a problem. When he really worked hard at it he could control it, but it seemed even the littlest bit of stress or frustration was too much. He'd gone to CVS and bought desensitizing cream, but it hadn't done much.

She took too long. He didn't take long enough. It was bound to start a fight.

THE BEDROOM DOOR OPENED. She came out in her coat and walked right past him, forgetting to stop and say goodbye. As an afterthought, she turned back and gave him a kiss on the cheek.

He got up, emptied his plate into the garbage and tossed it into the sink. Not hungry. In the living room, he found his tape on the shelf. He didn't even bother hiding it anymore. Into the slot of the VCR it went, and then, grabbing the remote from the top of the TV, he plopped onto the couch.

He fast-forwarded through the first two scenes, one girl on girl, the other a voyeuristic cleaning lady watching a silicone-enhanced brunette take it from behind. Prior to the fight, he hadn't watched this thing since he dubbed it from Dad's original back in college, on a trip home to do the laundry when no one was home. He hadn't had to. Sarah had always been adventurous enough to fulfill his wildest desires, but now it was different. She hadn't touched him below the belt in two weeks. They used to have sex as wild as the shit on this tape almost daily.

His favorite scene came up, a busty redhead servicing her man in the shower. He unzipped his pants and went to work.

The two of them on the screen made his love life pale by comparison. They may have been faking it, but that didn't matter. Less than a minute in, he lost interest. He clicked off the television set and lay back on the couch. Swallowed up by the heavy cushions, he began to cry.

૭૪૩

STEVE SAT THERE on his living room couch, pants unbuttoned, for about thirty minutes before getting up and brushing himself off. He looked around the room for his coat, sure he hadn't hung it up. It was on the chair. *I've got to get out.* Coat on. Keys in pocket. Out the door.

He pulled the coat close, hunching himself down into it, protecting himself from the bitter wind. He looked about. Their apartment was in the nice part of town, the Boston you saw on postcards and sitcoms, a sort of polished, phony bit of perfection buried deep within the grit and grime. The trees were Crayola green and the place reeked of disposable pine tree air fresheners, the kind he hung in his Camry. Everything about the neighborhood was just a gram of sugar too sweet. He didn't particularly like it. This was more Sarah's scene, the sweetness and the beauty.

He walked with no special destination in mind, no idea where he was going, when he would get there, or if he would ever come back. He shivered. The only source of warmth in his body was his crotch, and even the pulsing campfire in his loins was close to subsiding.

"You're looking rather cold tonight You need a place to crash?"

Steve looked around for the voice, the chill hitting his cheeks hard and reddening them. Beside him crept a toothpick of a man with no coat, only a T-shirt, patent leather pants, and a toothy grin covering him. Deep green eyes peered out from beneath a scraggly mane of magenta hair.

Steve searched the Toothpick's eyes. "Are you a Scientologist?"

"Why do you ask?"

"I had a friend once, got accosted by one of you guys, dragged into a building around here somewhere and forced to take all these tests."

"I'm not a Scientologist. I'm just a generous man offering you a place to stay."

"What's in it for you? Hoping to grab yourself an easy piece of ass?"

The Toothpick laughed, a big belly laugh that shouldn't have come from a man so small, with not a trace of a beer gut on him. "I'm not gay. And as for what's in it for me, well let's just say I enjoy helping folks like you out."

"Folks like me?"

"Lonely folks."

"How do you know I'm lonely?"

"The way you walk. The bulge in your pants." The Toothpick smirked.

"I'm married."

"Then you're worse off than I imagined," he snickered. "Some of the loneliest guys I've met on this street have been married men."

"I'm not lonely. I'm fine."

"How'd you like to be able to fuck your wife again?"

Steve stopped and gave him a hard stare. "Listen, pal, I don't know who you are or what you're up to, but I'm not listening to this bullshit, OK? My sex life is fine. I'm fine. I'm just taking a walk."

"OK, so you're sex life is fine. How'd you like to make it even better? How'd you like to give your wife an orgasm so good she'd do anything to please you afterward? And I do mean anything. Is there anything your wife won't do for you that you've always wanted to try?"

"No. She's an adventurous woman."

"She take it up the ass?"

Steve stopped and got in the guy's face. "You say shit like that about my wife one more time and I'll drop you man." He took a step back. "Got it?"

Steve was turned and ready to walk away when the Toothpick spoke again. "Would you like it if she took it up the ass?"

Steve swung his fist around at the Toothpick. This guy was going down. This guy was... out of the way. Steve stumbled over himself and fell to the ground.

"Would you like it if she took it up the ass?"

"She's my wife. I'm not gonna make her do anything she wouldn't want to do."

They stared each other down for a moment. The chill of the wind wasn't affecting Steve anymore. He was so hot, so mad. The Toothpick stood cool and confident, grinning like a madman. This guy was nuts. He didn't shiver at all as he continued his proposition. "Oh, but she would want to do it. Believe me she would do anything to have you, if you let me help you."

There was honesty in the guy's eyes, a scary, near-psychotic honesty, but truthfulness nonetheless. Despite his somewhat sleazy exterior, he had Steve convinced. "I just want her to touch me again," said Steve.

"Oh she'll touch you all right. Follow me." The Toothpick took the lead. Steve followed close behind.

࿓

STEVE FOLLOWED the Toothpick for what must have been at least thirty minutes down side street after side street, the ominous shadow of Copley Square and the Back Bay hanging over them, the Hancock tower and the Pru hunkering high above, then Comm. Ave., the bars, BU, and eventually the endless row of three story brick apartment buildings that crunched uncomfortably together all the way to Brighton. Steve and Sarah used to take walks like this, trying to get lost, just to see if they could find themselves again. They would always get back to their little hole in the wall with a smile on their faces for just having been together. Whatever this guy had to offer, it couldn't hurt.

"This is it." The Toothpick motioned to a ratty old townhouse. There was a young woman in a t-shirt and shorts standing outside smoking a butt. As they drew closer, Steve couldn't help but notice her nipples, rigid in the cold. *How can she stand out here wearing so little? She doesn't even have a bra on.* The Toothpick wrapped his arm around the young woman. "You like what you see?"

Steve replied, robotically, "I'm married."

The woman spoke. "That's not what he asked." She walked closer to Steve, tossing her butt on the ground and crushing it under her bare foot. "He asked if you liked what you saw."

She was gorgeous. No. Better than gorgeous. The t-shirt was

pulled tight over her thin little body. She wore no makeup, but somehow her face glowed. The flush of her cheeks, the pink of her lips, the light on her hair—it was like something out of a pinup calendar. The cutoffs she wore covered just enough skin to remain on this side of decency.

What about Sarah?

What about Sarah? She wasn't giving him what he needed. Maybe this little girl could.

"So, do you?" she asked.

The Toothpick was smoking a butt now. "I think the look on his face says it all. Maybe you should show him around, Cass?"

She smiled a perfect little smile. "I'd love to." She took his hand and led Steve into the house. "I didn't catch your name."

"It's Steve.

"Steven. I like that."

"No," he said. "It's Steve. Only my wife calls me Steven."

"I'll bet Steven turns you on, doesn't it?"

"Yeah."

"So why reserve it for your wife and no one else?"

"I... I don't know."

She smiled. "This is our house. Rick and I own the place. We house the lonely, give them a place to stay, occasionally the comfort of a woman or man."

"A whorehouse?"

"No." She giggled a bit. "We don't charge anything. Our friends, the men and women who live and work here, they do this because they enjoy making people feel good."

She lit another cigarette.

"You shouldn't smoke so much. It'll kill you."

"Smoking may kill you, Steven, but these things won't put a scratch on me." She blew a smoke ring, an obnoxious display that stirred the fading embers in his underpants. "I'm special," she informed him.

The temperature wasn't much warmer in the house, and the

people wandering back and forth through the foyer were wearing even less than Cass. He wished Cass were wearing less. Wearing nothing. He didn't understand what he was feeling, but he wanted this girl, more than he had ever wanted anything.

Just this once... would it be that bad? If my wife isn't going to give in to me, maybe this little thing will...

"Cass?"

"Yes, Steven."

His crotch throbbed and pulsed, and his mind raced unrestrained. "There anyplace a little more private we could go?"

She took his hand. "You *do* like what you see, don't you?"

He nodded. Then he scratched his scalp and pushed his hair back from his face. He felt sweat pooling on the small of his back. "I'd like to see more."

"Follow me." She pulled his hand and guided him up the stairs.

Such a perfect little ass. Like Sarah's... Forget about Sarah... this is better than anything Sarah has ever... Stop thinking...

The shorts were tight on her, and short, the kind someone only wears to get attention. Only a certain crop of women could get away with an outfit like this. She got away with it, and then some.

At the top of the stairs, grunts and moans filled the hall. People were enjoying themselves here, a far cry from the forced celibacy in his building. On the outside, it looked like a shack, but everything else about this place added to the mood, mirrors everywhere, lushly upholstered furniture, untarnished tables, a red rug the shade of untainted, freely flowing blood, a magnificently grotesque color.

"I think all the bedrooms are taken. How about in here?" She motioned to a bathroom.

"That'd be great."

"C'mon." She pulled him in. As the door slid shut she looked him up and down with a dirty glint in her eye. She was alive, boiling over with something, not like Sarah, who was empty and dead.

"I want to see more," he implored her.

She smiled, her hands unbuttoning the cutoffs. They dropped to the floor and there was nothing more to protect her, no underwear, just a small strip of red hair. Her t-shirt came off next, over her shoulders, revealing, releasing her breasts. He felt himself about to explode as she stood naked before him. She drew closer, her hands wandering over his chest, his backside, up and down his legs.

I can't stand it. I can't hold it.

"Look at that," she said. "You really do like what you see, don't you?"

He looked down, a huge stain expanding outward from his crotch. "I'm sorry."

She smiled. "Nothing to be sorry about. Why don't you get in the shower and wash off. I'll find you some new jeans."

"OK."

He pulled his shirt off and tossed it to the ground. *I can't believe it. Why am I even doing this? I can't last long enough to satisfy this girl.* He dropped his pants.

"Tightie whities, huh? Let me help you with those." She knelt and pulled them off for him. "Aren't they restricting?"

He felt himself blush, a wave of heat racing over him. "Sorry it's so small." He clenched his fist. Released.

"I've seen smaller." She stood up and led him into the shower. Pressing against him, she reached around to turn the shower on. The heat of her was intense. The water pounding against the back of his head felt good.

Look at her. Look at what I'm missing. Why can't I be strong enough to last?

She knelt down.

Looking for the soap probably.

She kissed his limp penis, flicked her tongue at it.

"It's useless. I won't be up for another twenty to thirty minutes. It's useles—"

"Let me be the judge of that, Steven."

She continued and she continued and just as he was about to pull her head away it happened, something that had never happened so fast for him. He was revived.

Steve looked down at his little vamp and she went to work, just like in his movie.

I'm not going to last. He was panting, his heart racing, but this time it didn't end. He didn't explode. It just kept building.

She worked on him for a good five minutes in this way, just like in the movie, and he was still there. He was lasting. He felt the corners of his mouth lift, an all to unfamiliar feeling over these past weeks.

Then the girl lay back in the tub. Had she seen that movie too? He'd told Sarah once about it, and of his fantasy to duplicate it, but the bathtub in their apartment was too small. This was eerie.

How could she know?

"Come inside me, Steven."

What about Sarah?

"Please come inside me, Steven."

This girl was unreal, the epitome of his sexual daydreams. His wife could only come close, as hard as she tried. This girl was pure fantasy brought to life, and so Steve mounted her, working away at her as the actor had done with the actress. The sensation was still building, but he was stronger now, strong enough to last. The girl surrendered under him, moaning his name.

Just like the movie.

Unreal.

She stopped him and they quickly rearranged themselves, without the awkward bumping around that seemed inevitable when he tried this with the other one. Cass faced the shower head on her hands and knees and Steve worked away at her with a speed and strength he had never been capable of. He felt possessed, compelled, by some force. Then, her body quaked around him, grabbed hold. His cock trembled and he was finished. Devoured. The shower pounded down on them.

"Sarah," he mumbled.

What am I doing? Who is this little girl I just... I just fucked... What about my wife? Get dressed. Get out of here.

"Sarah, oh God I'm sorry, what did I do?"

Find your pants!

She was out of the shower like a blur, her hands on him as he struggled to put on his shirt. Her fingertips slipped down into his pants.

So quick, this girl. As quick as the Toothpick. Impossibly so.

He was rising again as she dropped to her knees and unzipped him.

"Stop."

"I can't stop, Steven. And neither should you. You still like what you see, don't you?"

"I, I do, but I, I can't!" He pushed her away.

Zip your fly. Get out of here. I've got to get out of...

"I'm sorry, Cass. I never should have..."

Smiling up at him, she said, "No regrets, Steven. None. Never." She zipped up his pants.

⚅

DOWN THE STAIRS HE RAN. At the bottom, the women of the house blocked his escape, but he pushed his way through, throwing their prying, exploring hands off of him. He pushed his way out of that place and didn't look back. By the time he had reached his building, he should've been shivering. He hadn't had the chance to wipe off after the shower, and the crotch of his Levi's was soiled through. In spite of all this, he found himself hot. He hid his crotch with his jacket.

Please let Sarah be asleep. Or not back yet. Please God.

The door was ajar. Sarah stood by the coat rack. She hadn't noticed him and she was taking her coat off.

God, Sarah. I'm so sorry.

As the coat came off, the sweat on her naked skin glistened in the moonlight.

Naked? She's not wearing anything under the... What's going on here?

Steve shoved the door closed.

"Steven?" She spun around.

"What's going on, Sarah?"

She studied him and a look came to her eyes, a look he hadn't seen in weeks.

"Sarah?"

"Steven." She drew closer.

"Why weren't you wearing anything under your coat?"

"I was hoping to surprise you." Her hands slid down his chest.

What if she notices the stain? Oh God...

She unbuttoned his pants.

What if she sees?

If she saw, she did not say. She pushed his pants down to the ground and followed them as they fell, onto her knees. "It's been too long, Steven." His underwear was off, her mouth on him.

"Sarah, I, I've got to warn you, I—"

"Lets go to bed," she said, flicking her tongue at the tip of him one last time before standing. Her hand stroked him, and then grabbed him hard, leading him towards the bedroom. "Lets go to bed. I have some things I want to try."

HE LASTED LONGER than he had with Cass, which was the longest he'd lasted in his life, but still she was not satisfied. Under the covers she lay, with her back to him. Steve sat up, half proud of himself, and half disappointed that he had still not sated her.

"Is that all you have for me, Steven? It takes more than that to satisfy me. It takes—" She paused. "You always come so quick. I need you to last longer, Steven. Can't you work on it? Get some more of that desensitizing cream, a cock ring. Something."

"Sarah, I lasted an a full half hour. That's the longest I've ever—"

"Well, maybe that's not enough." She got up and crossed the room, staring out the small window that hung over her dresser.

His mouth hung open, his eyes wide. Steve got up, pulling his hair back as he neared her, his other fist clenched tight. He was hard again and it didn't cross his mind how odd that was. He was inside of her with one violent thrust. She leaned on that bureau and thrust herself backward to take him in.

"Oh God, Steven."

❦

THOUGH IT TOOK MORE to satisfy her, their sex life returned to normal, and stayed that way for the better part of a month. They'd take a shower together in the morning, extra early to allow for sex, and then there was the reprise right after dinner at least four times a week. They'd even met for lunch a couple of times for quickies. Of the two of them, he was the one getting tired of it. He was stuffed. She always begged for more, for seconds and thirds. He tried not to mind. This was the best their sex life had been.

But something was still different. Sarah's eyes continued to lack that certain something. She had become something of a machine, for which he was now the fuel. They'd make love at least once a day, sometimes twice, but it wasn't really making love. It was fucking. Back in college, he'd had this theory that there were three different types of sex. There was 'fucking,' which was basically two people getting off with each other, fulfilling that basic need. There was 'having sex,' which involved two people who kind of felt something. Then there was 'making love.' Not many people got around to 'making love.'

So while his libido loved the change of pace, his heart still ached. "I'm done, Steven. Are you ready for dessert?"

"Didn't you get your period yesterday?"

"Yeah, but I don't care. It's a light flow, and the cramps are all but gone."

"You know I don't like doing that."

She paused, stared at the cupboards.

"Sarah?"

"What am I doing wrong, Steven? Don't you want me?" She unbuttoned her blouse. "Don't you want this, Steven? I want you so."

"Can't we just take a few days off?"

She crawled to him on all fours and lapped at his crotch as if it were a saucer of milk. "Don't you like what you see?"

He ground his teeth. "Of course I like what I see, dear. I just don't feel up to it right now."

She stood up. "Maybe I should go find someone else, like you did that night."

She did notice?

Sarah blushed, wrapped her arms around herself, and turned away from him. "I'm sorry," she said. "I just thought... Forget it. I'm going to bed."

"Sarah?" He went after her, but it was useless. The bedroom door slammed shut in his face.

Fuck. He grabbed his keys off of the table.

He was down the stairs in a matter of moments, slamming the door behind him, passing Nigel, and Sam, and Mrs. Henderson without saying hello, not paying attention to their advice that maybe he should get a coat. *I don't want to deal with this bullshit. The sex is fine now, but she's still fucked up. I don't know what to do.*

"Where you going in such a hurry?" asked a familiar voice as he descended the steps. He looked up from his anger. It was Cass. "How are you?" she asked.

"Good," he informed her.

"How's the wife?"

"Long story."

"You wanna talk about it?"

"That depends. You gonna try to get down my pants?"

"No. I've been fed today."

"Oh. Who fed you?"

"Rick. Then he pissed me off. So I decided to take a walk."

"Aren't you cold in that?" Same as before, nothing but a t-shirt and cutoff jean shorts in the middle of February.

"Why? You wanna warm me up?"

"No. Actually, I think I'm through with sex for a while."

She smiled her little smile, that devious, sleazy grin. "That's what you say now. You'll be aching for it in a few hours. That's the way we are."

"Not all human beings are sex fiends. You and my wife might be—"

"Sex gives you something though, doesn't it? A little charge. You can't deny that."

"I can deny it," he said. "Right now, sex doesn't give me anything. It takes away. It drains me."

"I don't think you're being truthful with yourself."

"What do you mean?"

"Are you sure that it's draining, and not filling?"

"Sex is anything but filling. Sex is all about release and loss."

"That's an awful way to look at something so fun."

'Sure, it's fun while it's going on, but afterward, it's like I've lost a part of myself."

She walked and he followed without questioning it. "Well, technically, you're right. As a man, you do lose part of yourself. But are you trying to tell me you don't enjoy it in the slightest?"

"Sometimes, but not often."

"Did you enjoy it when you were with me?"

"Yeah. I did."

"Maybe it's just your wife."

Steve stopped but Cass kept walking, tossing only the briefest glance back to see what he was doing.

"Don't act so shocked. I'm not going to censor myself just to please you."

"Maybe I don't want to talk to you if you're going to say things like that."

"Of course you're going to talk to me. We're going to talk all the way back to my place and then you're going to fuck me."

"Excuse me?"

"You want to. You need to."

"I thought you said you weren't going to try and get down my pants."

"I'm not." She came back to him, drew closer. "But you look me in the eyes and tell me you can resist. Go ahead, Steven."

Steve was silent. Cass began to walk again, and like a lapdog, like her own personal little bitch, Steve followed close behind.

☙❧

HE LAY on his back as Cass cleaned him off with her tongue. Steve wondered why he had done it again. His stomach, his crotch, his whole body answered him. It was filling, a three-course meal. Sarah was like fast food lately. Sarah was McDonalds, or, on a good day, Wendy's. Cass was the Outback Steakhouse, not quite classy—more of a sawdust on the floor kind of gal—but filling, and finger-licking good just the same.

Cass slinked up his body, her tongue gliding up from his crotch to his Adam's apple. She wrapped herself around him, as if to leech back the energy he had stolen from her. Sarah did that too. She never had enough. Neither of them ever did. It was something he had found true with all of the women he had been with. He was satisfied after one time, maybe two. They always wanted more.

The thing was, he was obligated to give Sarah more by the ring on his finger. He was bound and chained to serve her, but he could just get up and leave when he was done with Cass.

Maybe that's why he had done it again.

"I guess you didn't give up sex after all, Steven."

"Where's the Toothpick?"

"The who?"

"Rick."

"The Toothpick?" She smirked. "I've never heard anyone call him that. It is pretty fitting." She pulled a Marlboro from the near-empty pack on the nightstand. "I don't know where he is."

Steve gently pushed Cass away as he sat up. Cass turned onto her side, away from him. "What?" he asked.

"That's it? You don't want more?"

"No." He found his pants on the floor. "I think I've had enough."

"Going back to the little woman?"

"I think so." *Good.* He thought, stepping into his shoes. *Completely dressed and she didn't even try anything.*

"Well, I'm sure I'll see you around."

"Don't be so sure, Cass. I've made this mistake twice now. I don't intend on making it again."

"Third time's the charm," she said, puffing away.

He stared at her naked body. Such perfect curves. Such a tight little ass. His little fix. Maybe he would be back. Maybe he would *have* to come back.

He remembered a time way back when, when that sort of thing wouldn't have even mattered to him. It wasn't that long ago, was it? He hadn't fallen for Sarah because of her body. God knows he didn't complain about the way she looked in a tight pair of jeans, but what hooked him on her was her voice, and her eyes. Her curves were just a bonus. Now, curves seemed to be all that mattered. As he crept cautiously down the stairs, he caught himself letting a tear go. He rubbed his eyes, erased any trace it from his face, and descended back into the city.

⚜

STEVE MADE his way to the apartment building quicker than he had before. At least it seemed that way. Perhaps it was because he was thinking so hard about what was going on, but then again, he always thought hard.

He remembered back in college before he met Sarah, how he dreamed of sex, of getting laid ten times a night like one of the guys in his porno. When they did finally get together, and finally started having sex, it was great. All his hornball aggressions came out. He never thought he'd become disinterested in it, but he had.

No, it wasn't disinterest. It was that he didn't have enough energy. She'd wanted it more, but he was working, stressing. His energy was down. But that didn't matter. She always wanted it, every ounce of him that wasn't spread thin somewhere else. He had nothing left for himself.

⚜

IT WASN'T until he was at the door with his key in the lock that he heard her. There was moaning coming from inside the apartment. He pressed his ear to the door. *Who? Who is she with? How could she?* He turned the knob slowly. *I'll kick his ass. Whoever he is.*

As the door swung open, Steve stood ready to attack, to defend, but there was no one there, no one but Sarah, strewn across the couch with her clothes strewn across the floor, one hand running over the length of her body, the other working away between her legs.

He closed the door. Her ears were fixed on the music issuing from the stereo, and on her own sounds, so she did not hear him.

The music always made it that much more romantic to her, that much more complete. He watched her as she continued, body trembling, sweat glistening on her, catching the light of the flickering candle.

She wasn't very loud. He'd been with a screamer right before he met her and it was all an act. Sarah's sounds were so much more real. She moaned softly, the intensity rising, but seldom the volume. He watched her there, fulfilling her needs herself, and felt suddenly and utterly useless.

When she was done, she lay there soft and silent. The tear that he had wiped away at Cass's returned, but this time he could not hold it back. There was a smile on her face. For the first time in a month, there was a smile on her face. She sighed lightly and her chest rose and fell in a slow, intoxicating rhythm.

She doesn't need me. I need her, but she doesn't need me.

His eyes filled with a potent mixture of tears and of her. She was at once the most gorgeous and most painful thing he had ever seen.

SYLVIA'S MASTERPIECE

She felt the warmth of the sun spill over her. She had nothing to hide behind. No battle gear. No war paint. Just her body, naked on the bed, the purple satin sheets and floral print down comforter twisted chaotically and pushed aside from the night before. The sun's caress was a slow one, a lover who took his time, starting with her feet and working his way up, an exquisite solar massage that pushed every bit of last night's escapade out of her pores.

She was hesitant to open her eyes. The sight of the light would not be nearly as pleasant as the feel of it. Her hand traced the contours of the bed searching for him, but he was gone. She let her hand rest there for a moment and sighed.

Half of her body ached to rise, and the other half begged to stay. She hadn't been able to lie like this, to be alone in forever. It was some kind of blessing in disguise that he took his sticks and ran. Now she could just lay here, the heat purging her in a slow, comfortable sweat.

When the sun grew to be too much and the bathroom called to her, she forced open her eyes and let the light fill them. She sat up, and it was slow motion, everything about her moving at half its normal speed. Her hands searched the bed again, this time for her battle gear. She smiled to herself, realizing she might never find something that small amongst all this. It was a little black number. Tight. Accentuated all the right curves. It was one of her favorites for exactly that reason. The boys and girls couldn't help but stare. But the apartment was empty. The only gaze she had to meet was the security camera outside the main door. Today the heavy breathing was nothing more than the heaving sigh of the air conditioner. With no one to watch her, she didn't really need the slinky thing. What would be the point?

She moved across the room with relish. She hadn't done this since she was in college, frolicked about with nothing to protect her. Work was so intense, so ingrained in her. It was impossible to be this carefree about her appearance with a camera documenting every step of her strut, and every strand of her hair. She glanced occasionally at the dozens of framed magazine covers that ordained her wall. She didn't have to be her today, the Sylvia that every horny young boy over the age of thirteen knew and masturbated to.

In the bathroom, she released the final remnants of last night's madcap jaunt. The shower beckoned her, and it would have been the next logical step, the next segment of her carefully planned day, but she didn't feel the need. Today she would wear the sweat. There were no noses here to seduce with lavish perfumes.

She returned to her bedroom alive in a way that she had hoped would come with Scott last night. But Scott had been, like most drummers, nothing more than the rhythm, nothing more than the driving beat of his songs. Scott made her come. She couldn't deny that. But he did it systematically, methodically. No emotion. How had she ended up with the drummer anyway? She had always been strictly L.V.; lead vocalists were it. They and their egos were always a pain in the ass, but they were also undeniably the best in bed. They were the emotion, the passion of the group, and they brought that lust for amazing performances into the boudoir.

JOHNNY BAPTIST HAD BEEN the best of the best. All vocalists had egos, but not even a handful had something to back those egos up. Johnny did. Johnny wasn't the guy who'd gotten the drunken crowd cheering at the karaoke bar one day and decided to get himself a band together. He'd studied at Berklee. Yes he'd dropped out, but then again, most of the talent at Berklee dropped out unless they were into jazz. Johnny did two years, and he was magnificent, beyond par. The teachers knew it. His fellow students knew it. Sylvia knew it the moment she spotted him that night downstairs at the Middle East.

Sylvia was in her second year at UMass Boston when she met him. Psych major. Art therapy. Johnny joked that psych majors were just girls who couldn't decide what they wanted to be coming out of high school, and couldn't bring themselves to say they were "undecided." A couple of friends had dragged her to see the annual Battle of the Bands thing that WBCN hosted every year. She wasn't into the rock scene, but they promised her this band was amazing.

"They're called what?"

"Q."

"Q?"

"Mmm hmm."

"I certainly hope their music is more inspired than the name."

"Cynic."

"Forgive me for not wanting to throw away the ten bucks I have left over from work-study after paying the bills for a band named Q. I'm not even into this grungy mope-rock bullshit."

"Q is not mope rock, Sylvia. They're goth and they're brilliant."

"Brilliant?"

"Ugh."

Despite any preconceived notions, Sylvia fell in love with him right then and there, the moment she descended the final step into the murky darkness of the club's lower level. Her friends spotted him in the crowd and said, "That's the lead singer. Isn't he gorgeous?" If their music was even half as good as he looked... His firm ass was held hostage by glossy black vinyl. A tight crimson turtleneck left no part of his chiseled pecs to the imagination. The hair, she could do without. Scraggly was the only word for it. It was an inch and a half too long and dyed jet black. But then, hidden beneath his mane, there was that face. Men shouldn't be allowed to have such pretty faces.

She was as pleasantly surprised by the music as she was by the singer's dashing good looks. This was not the crap that her friends seemed desperately, hopelessly attached to. This was clever music, clever music with a heart, and a pulse. Synthesizers, guitars, and the wail of a banshee boiled and bubbled and brewed together in the witch's cauldron of that club; he was the warlock, stirring the broth, splashing the onlookers with it, drawing them all in.

SYLVIA CROSSED to her stereo and turned the knob from zero to ten with a quick flick of her wrist. She danced around the apartment and sang off-key into the remote control as if it were her own little microphone. Her body flailed and swung, twist and turn, and moved with determination to the beat, invoking the soul of the Material Girl herself, as she and the CD sang together, "C'mon girls! Do you believe in love? 'Cause I got somethin' to say about it, and it goes somethin' like this." She had the body and the moves and she thought, was it not for her voice, she might actually have been able to make a career at this.

Four songs later, she collapsed onto the bed, staring up into her eyes in the mirror that hung above. It had spooked Scott out, to the point that for a few seconds he actually seemed a being of flesh and blood, instead of an icy fuck machine.

"What?" she'd said. "Why'd you stop?"

Panting, he said, "You've got a mirror above your bed."

"You've never seen a mirror hanging above a bed? I refuse to believe that."

"I've just never seen one above a woman's bed. Makes a certain statement."

SHE LOOKED UP AT HERSELF, at the flat stomach, the ample breasts, and of course, the authentic blonde hair cropped at her shoulders. She rolled onto her side, and there was the ass that most of her co-workers would kill or fuck a plastic surgeon for. There was a lot to be thankful for, a lot of body to feel blessed for having, but she couldn't avoid her eyes. Johnny had immortalized them in song, calling them, "deep blue," but they never seemed deep enough to her.

Hundreds of thousands of men bought things because of those breasts, that tight body, that gorgeous backside every day, either for themselves, in the form of posters, magazines, or videos, or in the form of scarcely-there underwear for their wives, girlfriends, and mistresses. She was willing to bet that none of them bought a damn thing because of her eyes.

She sat up, pulling herself from the reflection. Every trace of Scott was gone, but still he haunted her. Sleeping with him had brought back something. The other girls never thought about this, she was convinced. They were as comfortable in the stereotype as they were naked on the couch of casting director. Maybe they did think about these things and they just didn't tell anyone, or maybe the cash was just too comforting to notice, the attention to addictive to give up. Sylvia had shared her bed with countless men, and never woken to the introspection that was plaguing her now.

Scott had done it. He had brought about all of these feelings. It was Scott and the mirror. Had he expected her to be as shallow and one dimensional as her reflection? For him, she guessed, the only part of her that needed to be real was the part between her legs. That was all the reality he wanted.

Most men looked at her like that, looked at her as they did her billboards, her magazine spreads. What was the difference with Scott? Sylvia pushed herself back and leaned against the headboard. She pulled her knees to her chin and wrapped her arms about herself. He had made her feel that way. Others had tried to relegate her to that role, but she had always been in control. She had always known who she was, and that had been her secret weapon against them, against their attempts to compress the layers of her. But Scott had been in control last night with his unbreakable rhythm, with the methodical look in his eyes, and the way in which he impaled her. There was a look in his eyes when he let go inside of her: emptiness, hollowness. He was a horny sixteen-year-old fucking his pillow. Silent. Quick. Emotionless.

She untangled the covers and pulled them over herself. A tear sat on her long lashes ready to slip down her cheek. Maybe they had all been like that. She hadn't bothered to look into their eyes since Johnny. The tear slipped free. Nobody's eyes could compare to Johnny's. She remembered how he used to lay his head in her lap after they made love. He would stare up at her like a child, mystified by her. She would run her fingers through his hair, losing herself in him, and the way he got lost in her.

"Sylvia?"

"Yeah?"

"You were spacing."

"Was I?"

He nodded.

"I was just thinking."

"About what?"

She couldn't find the words.

"That same thing?"

She nodded.

"You're a good model."

"But that's all I am, Johnny. Do I really want to be an image for people to drool over?"

"There's a lot more to you than that. Modeling is just your job."

"I want to create something. Like you." She paused. "And don't feed me the 'eventually when you have children' line."

"I wasn't going to say—"

"It's like Richard Gere," she said, adding, for clarification, "in *Pretty Woman*. Julia Roberts asks him what his company makes and he can't answer, cause he doesn't make anything."

"This is only important to you because you're dating me."

"That's not true."

"I've been with girls who, when they're with me, have decided they have this need to be creative all of a sudden. They think creativity is this brilliant problemless thing."

"That's not why I want to create. I..."

He got up and slid to the edge of the bed. He was searching for his pants.

"I want to create because—"

"Because why Sylvia? Because why?"

She turned from him.

"Sylvia, it's not all it's cracked up to be. Sometimes I would give anything to be working behind a desk pushing fucking buttons every day."

"You have this way of releasing. I envy it."

"Creating isn't only about releasing. You can release just as well with a box of Kleenex."

SHE SEARCHED FOR A TISSUE. It had been their first fight, not a knock-down, drag-out affair by any means, but it was enough. He took off that night. Q had a record deal. They saw less and less of each other. It wasn't on purpose. He wasn't mad at her. At least she didn't think he was. They "drifted apart," and she heard from him every once in a while. They got together once, when she started doing runway shows in Manhattan. The sex was amazing, but he'd gotten into heroin, to ease his pain, and that wasn't her scene. She never understood what pain he was trying ease. He died a couple of days later outside of their old apartment in the Back Bay in Boston. The sweet old landlady found him. Sylvia could still hear the tiny crack in Mrs. Henderson's voice the night she called with the news.

Her career got a little boost from it. She started appearing all over the talk show circuit as the girl who inspired Q's one and only love song. There were hundreds of magazine interviews floating out there with somber pictorials of her visiting their favorite spots, and curled up with old things of his she'd kept hold of: a teddy bear in a leather jacket he'd gotten her for Valentine's day; the notebook in which he'd written the band's biggest hit, "Divine Hatred." One of those innumerable articles caught the attention of the Masterpiece people, manufacturers of skimpy undergarments for the sophisticated. She had just the right "sensitivity" for the campaign.

She had to find the damn Kleenex.

She searched the apartment high and low, tears running down her cheeks, spilling onto the rest of her, and speeding along the dangerous curves of her body, Johnny singing "and I spin and I swerve along her dangerous curves" to her in a daydream. She sniffled, felt her nose dripping. If anyone saw her now... She ended her quest with the closet, and there were no tissues there either.

She collapsed against the open door, and a few random things fell loose from the pile of junk opposite the heaps of shoeboxes stacked to the right. She sifted through the pile. Most of it consisted of old magazines and books, but amongst the mess she saw something she hadn't seen in ages, her black sketchbook. She flipped through it slowly. There lay page after page of her life drawings: still drawings of pears and apples and oranges, then nudes. Quick thirty-second ones. She remembered how much she hated those, how awkward-looking the male model had been, how his penis shriveled up in the drafty art studio. Then there were the doodles, and the caricatures of her classmates. She had carried this thing with her everywhere, drew everything. She'd never shown him these. Drawing teacher killed her desire to draw a few months before she first met Johnny. Told her she would find more success as the model than as the artist.

She really needed the Kleenex now. She sifted through more of the garbage in her closet, but there were no tissues. As she wiped the tears from her face she found quite an odd thing: a box of old Crayola crayons and an envelope. She opened it and slid the colorful Hallmark card out. It was from Mrs. Henderson. When had she given her this?

A smile crept across her face as she read it, "Teachers and boyfriends don't know everything dear. Especially men. Never give up. You've got a masterpiece in you, dear. We all do. –Emily Henderson"

The Crayolas sat half open at her feet. They were only crayons, but they would do.

She took the crayons and the sketchbook, sat on the bed, and began to draw. The tears fell on the pages now, alongside the crayon. It was eleven pages of doodling before she got back into it, and then she just couldn't stop. Sylvia sat on her bed drenched in the sunlight, covered with crayon dust, and she drew. She drew.

DEUX EX MACHINA

I met the woman who changed my life at a library. I suppose that makes me sounds like a total dork, but I'm really not. My wife is reading over my shoulder, laughing.

Alright, I concede. I am a bit of a dork. I graduated from Kimball College in the spring of 1998, summa cum laude. I majored in science while I was there, even though the school was primarily known for its arts department. I studied for my master's at a slew of different places before finally giving up. None of them quite suited me. A huge pharmaceutical company got a hold of one of my papers, though. They—*you*—made me an offer I couldn't refuse. And, well, that's basically it. I've been here ever since. But all that's about to change.

You see, sir, this is my letter of resignation. I am writing to you because I no longer wish to waste my life away at something that doesn't matter all that much, something that shouldn't even be done at all. If I were working on cloning organs for diseased patients or something like that, maybe this would all be different. But what we're working on is pointless, and I desire more in life than pointless pursuits.

The woman I met in the library wasn't my wife. I met my wife at Kimball, back in the day, at brunch one Sunday morning, arguing over whether the bacon was good or not. She likes hers soggy; I like mine crisp. No, the woman that I met in the library, the one that changed my life, was someone else, someone totally different, a nice old lady with quite a story to tell.

It was a cold October day, though Todd Gross had reported it would be in the mid-seventies by the afternoon. I've always trusted that Todd Gross, ever since the no-name storm back in '92. He's the best meteorologist in Boston if you ask me. Todd said it would be warm later, but sitting on that train as it pulled out of Acton station, hunched over my laptop with my coat pulled tight around me, I was a bit doubtful. Todd had never been exceptionally off the mark, but at that moment, as my fingers trembled on the keys, adding extra semicolons to the report I was working on, I wasn't seeing mid-seventies in my near future.

The first half of that day slagged along as I sat through meeting after meeting with the bigwigs who had come down from headquarters in Burlington. I had to resist asking, as I always did, what the hell the company was thinking building their headquarters in the middle of the woods of Vermont when all the big meetings happened down here. I had to resist the urge to tell them that the project was going nowhere, that my archaeologist friend had not yet provided the piece of cloth we needed, that he was having second thoughts. They didn't want to hear that. You didn't want to hear that.

When noon finally came, I took flight from the office with my black binder. How many times sir, have you asked me what was in that binder and been frustrated when my answer was "stuff"? Well, I'm going to tell you what's in the binder because it's crucial to the story. You ready? It's really exciting.

In my black binder, I keep two years worth of genealogy research. That's right, more research. You'd think I'd be bored researching this and that all day, that I wouldn't want to waste my lunch hour researching even more, but this research is different.

In fact, the big difference is that this research means something. It helps me to get connected with my past, to discover things about where I've come from, which'll maybe help me figure out where I'm going.

With my black binder stuffed into my coat and my hands stuffed deep into two of the half dozen pockets I had to choose from in the jacket I was wearing, I steered my way through Copley Square towards Newbury Street. A few blocks away from our office, on Newbury, is the New England Historic Genealogical Society. Their offices and library reside in a seven-story brick building wedged between trendy restaurants and fashion boutiques.

My favorite floor is the fourth floor. That's where they keep all of their microfilm records. Half of the floor is well lit, and centers around a reception and help desk area. There are bookcases filled to the brim with indexes for all manner of records, and there are tables lining the wall by the windows. A couple of mid-level PCs sit over there too, with genealogical software on them. Another quarter of the room is taken up by the actual filing cabinets themselves, where all the microfilm rolls are kept, stored individually in hard cardboard boxes about three inches wide by three inches tall. Some are thicker than others.

The last quarter of the room is dark and rather foreboding, at least to the uneducated soul. The first time I saw it, I felt a little bewildered. That last quarter of the room is where the microfilm readers are. Some are powered by electricity, others by the flick of your wrist. I prefer those hand-powered ones. They're less noisy, and it seems to me that when you're delving into the past in the way that you do in a place like that, it makes sense to use the more natural, more archaic equipment.

I mention all this because I think it's very important to set the scene for you. You've got to know what this place looked like. You've got to know, because if you see it the way I see it then you'll understand that I should've seen something mysterious and magical coming a mile away. That place is eerie and things happen there.

I was turning the hand-crank slowly, my eyes locked on the white panel the machine projected its image upon. Census records were the business of the day. You see, census records are useful because once you're back to a certain point, there is no one alive who can tell you how many brothers and sisters my great-great-great-grandfather Chuck had. You have to go back and look at the official records. They'll tell you that he had six brothers and three sisters, and if you look carefully enough you'll even discover that he had a seventh brother who died young, before any of the others were born.

You can find a lot out from looking at the old censuses. They were always changing what kind of information they gathered. Censuses are great for genealogists, even ones like me who have to ask for help with the old handwriting about once every twenty minutes.

The pace was slow because I had no idea where the guy I was looking for was. As it happened, my great-great-grandfather— good ole Chuck's son—was estranged from his wife near the end of his life and he went and lived someplace in Boston. He was estranged from his son too, my great grandfather, and so nobody knows where the hell he was those last years, except that he died in the Boston Sanatorium sometime in 1925.

On his death record, which I had to travel out to Dorchester to get—do you remember that morning I didn't come in till 11:45 and you thought it quite peculiar because I had never been tardy in my entire ten-month tenure?—it said nothing more than what I already knew, that he died at the sanatorium of complications from benign prostatic hypertrophy. It did give a few additional details about a catheter he had to use, details that no one really needed, not even me.

There weren't any relatives in Boston. The family had started out there, there and in Plymouth, back in the early 1600s, but our branch of it had taken up residence primarily in Harwich, down the Cape. Fishermen and carpenters for two hundred and fifty years, we hardly moved until all the estrangements started happening in the late eighteen hundreds. In the 1930s, when he was old enough to start making decisions for himself, my own grandfather fled the chaos of his family on the Cape like his grandfather Jim before him and moved out to midwestern Massachusetts, out here to Acton. There wasn't any reason for great-great grandpa Jim to be in Boston, but the records said he was.

"Who you looking for?" came the voice from the microfilm reader next to me.

I looked up from my reader to see who it was. Sitting in the chair to my right was a frail old lady, must've been near a hundred years old; she wore a hard-won smile on her weathered but pretty face.

"My great-great-grandfather. He, he moved to Boston in his later years, but nobody's sure where. I'm trying to get a fix on him."

"Have you checked boarding houses?"

"That's what I'm doing now. I'm keeping an eye out."

"There was a rather large one, when I was a small girl, in the North End. Ninety-nine percent Italian, of course, but he might've been there."

"Where was that?"

"The North End." The lady stood up, steadying herself on the chair. She reached over me and turned the hand crank. "You were almost there yourself." She turned it a bit more. "What was his name?"

"Jim... uh, James. James Bassett."

The lady stood up and pointed down at the image floating on the white projection panel, light as air. "There you are."

And she was right. I smiled. Right there, before my eyes, was the name I had been looking for. James L. Bassett. My great-great grandfather.

"How did you...?"

"How could I dear?" She smiled. "It was just a hunch."

The kind old lady returned to her research and I returned to mine. I had thirty more minutes before I had to get back to work and I spent all of them staring at this image, copying down every bit of information it relayed about James L. Bassett and also, everything it revealed about the people who ran the house he lived in. If there's anything I've learned about genealogy, it's that you never overlook a possible connection. Sure, I'd never heard of an Emily Henderson before, but if my great-great-grandfather was living under her roof, for even a few weeks, there was a possibility I would hear from her again.

When the thirty minutes had passed, I shut off my film reader, returned the microfilm and its box to the appropriate drawer, and headed towards the elevator. The lady who helped me was already there and she held the door for me even though it took most of her strength to do so.

As we began our descent she asked me, "Did you find everything you were looking for?"

"I did."

The elevator stopped and we waited for the door to open but it did not. I looked over at the indicator. It still read '4.'

"I think we're stuck." I told her.

She nodded her head and the grin did not disappear from her face. It was good that she wasn't panicked. I was panicked enough for the both of us. I don't like enclosed spaces. My armpits were already moist and the pit of my back was collecting the droplets that ran down into it.

"Jeremy," she began.

"How did you know my name?"

"I've been watching you."

"I have a ninety-year-old stalker?"

"No, Jeremy," she laughed. "You have a ninety-five-year-old guardian angel."

"I don't need a guardian angel, do I?" I said, chuckling nervously. "Aren't guardian angels for people who are in trouble, for kids with cancer or something? I don't have cancer, do I?"

"Not that I know of," she said. "But I'm not a doctor."

I backed up against the wall furthest from her. I didn't understand why we weren't moving yet. The elevator couldn't really be stuck, could it?

"Jeremy, please relax. I have only a few things to share with you and then we'll be on our way."

I sunk down the side of the elevator till I sat on the floor of it. I pressed the emergency button, and the intercom, but they did nothing. My mouth felt dry and I wished a little of the moisture that was pouring out of my pores elsewhere would filter on up to my throat.

"Jeremy, I have been a guardian angel for one hundred years. In that time, I have aged only ten years. I thought it strange that an angel would age at all, but I never let it bother me. It's really all the same after 95 anyway. After 95, you're on God's good humor.

"You see, Jeremy, I come from the future."

I cut her off. "Wait. You're an angel *and* you come from the future?"

"Please let me finish."

"Sorry."

"I come from the future, Jeremy, from a time when Christ has been reborn on Earth."

I imagine that at that point my jaw hung open as far as it would, that I looked like a codfish, recently caught, his eyes bulging from the lack of proper breathing, his mouth wide. How could she know about our project, sir? How?

"A speck of blood was found on an old piece of the Shroud of Turin, a piece that had been in private hands for centuries, apart from the rest of it, from the main piece which lay in a museum somewhere.

"From the speck of blood, a human fetus was cloned, and

implanted into a mother chosen in a worldwide search. Word spread fast of what was happening, and holy wars were threatened across the globe. This was blasphemy. No one would stand for it.

"Nine months passed and the child was born, and thus began a golden age, or so we thought.

"Peoples of all religions, races, creeds, they united over this child and he came to rule us all. Those who had trusted science all along were reaffirmed. Those who had never trusted it were converted. Science became the religion of all peoples, the religion that child preached from the moment he could talk.

"Soon, instead of praying, we were sticking needles into our necks, to extract the very root of sin itself, a chemical in our brains. All seemed to be well. But there is always a calm before the storm.

"One fine morning there was an explosion at the facility where the chemicals we extracted from ourselves were kept. From that explosion arose a beast that terrorized the city. This is New York City I'm speaking of. At that time, I was living in Manhattan.

"The beast was finally stopped by a dear boy named Samuel, a dear, dear boy. He was an atheist and he had never had the sin taken from his body. Because of this he was the only one who could withstand the pure evil of that creature, and God bless him, he gave his body and his soul to save the rest of us."

"Where was Christ during all of this?"

"In his citadel. Watching."

"Why wasn't he down there helping? He was born to be the savior wasn't he?"

"You can clone a body, Jeremy, but not a soul."

"What happened next?"

"I do not know. That night, I lay down with a heavy heart. I wanted nothing to do with that world. I longed to be in my husband's arms again. He had passed on twenty years before, and though I had always been a strong woman, there was not enough strength in me to deal with that world. I laid down and I never woke up."

I looked up at her in wonder. This story was too much. I mean... it made sense. All of my fears about this project of ours... she was speaking to all of them. But she could've simply been imaginative. She could be making it all up. If somehow she found out about our project, it is possible that she could extrapolate upon that and create this horrible vision. Couldn't she?

"I never woke up there that is, unless this is all a dream and I have yet to come around. I'm not sure this is a dream, though. I, I —there has to have been some purpose to what has happened to me."

"What has happened to you?"

"When next I woke it was almost a hundred and thirty years earlier. I had been sent back in time by someone, or something, back beyond my own birth, beyond even my parents', or even my grandparents' births. I actually arrived two months before either of them was born, in the year 1900.

"For the next hundred or so years I did as I felt God wanted me to do. I ran boarding houses, including the one your great-great-grandfather stayed at during those last years; later, I ran apartment complexes across the country, in Los Angeles, and New York, and, most recently, back here in Boston, in the Back Bay. My tenants, they have always been a feisty bunch. Quite a few amazing adventures among them.

"I did my best to help all those who I came in contact with. I did my best to help them through the dark times."

"That was very good of you."

"But it wasn't necessary."

"Excuse me?" I pushed myself up from the floor and stood eye to eye with her. "In the world we live in, good Samaritans are always welcome."

"But I wasn't a Samaritan. I was the hand of God. A Samaritan's advice is based on their own personal experiences, and their help is the help of a fellow human being. My help was the help of God. We were meddling. We knew everything about their situations and we pushed them in the right direction instead of giving them the information and letting them decide for themselves."

"Some people need pushing."

She shook her head. "What I've realized is that angels, that the hand of God, they aren't necessary. He created man in is own image. Man can, and will, figure it out for himself."

She took my hand in her own and it didn't occur to me to take it back.

"God has faith in us."

"Then why'd he let you become an angel?"

"So I could see for myself, so I could see that people don't need angels. They just need confidence. God made the world a well-oiled machine. It will work out its kinks by itself. There is no need for a deus ex machina."

"A what?"

"God in the machine." She looked at me inquisitively and I felt as though her eyes were burning holes into my own, looking for some sort of recognition.

"I'm surprised that, as an educated man, as a man educated at a school known for its theatre department, you never ran across the concept of deus ex machina."

"What is it?"

"In the Greek theatre there was a machine, a sort of crane, which at the end of a show would lower a god or goddess into the fray to solve all of the problems that the writer had worked up. It was referred to as a deus ex machina."

"And you see yourself as a deus ex machina as well?"

"You are my last attempt at it."

"What do you want from me?" I asked her.

"I know of your research, Jeremy. You are the one who will bring about the second Christ, but you have a chance to stop it."

"You don't want me to move forward with the research."

"No. I don't want you to move forward with the research. I've seen what happens. The world will not be better off for it, Jeremy. I know that's what you're hoping but... It simply will not work."

"If I don't head up this project, if I tell them no, I'll lose my job."

"And you're worried about your wife—"

"And the child."

The elevator lurched and Emily and I stumbled into each other's arms as it shook and began again to descend.

"Thank the Lord," I said aloud, not thinking of what message my jubilation might convey. "I hate enclosed spaces," I quickly appended.

Emily hugged me and whispered in my ear, just before the doors opened. "Do what you must, but please think about what I've told you."

She was out the door in a hurry, as fast as her old legs would take her, and I would have followed if the clerk at the front desk hadn't stopped me to inquire about renewing my membership.

I did as she said and thought about it for a few days. It was hard to sleep. Maureen was wondering what was wrong. She was supposed to be the one up all night. She was supposed to be the one throwing up in the morning and craving pickles and deviled ham in the middle of the night. I guess I only just decided for sure a few minutes ago.

You see, she—Emily—was wrong. Every once in a while, I think we do need a little help from the Guy upstairs, whether through angels, or priests, or whatever. I don't know if I would have made this choice if she hadn't been stuck in that elevator with me that day.

She was wrong about that, but she was right about something else. People don't need a God on Earth, an actual physical God. They don't need a clone of their beloved Christ to lead them towards a new era of peace and harmony. They don't need what we were going to give them. The hand of God is in all of us. The strength of God is in all of us. We just need to see it, and when we do, life will be so much better.

He has faith in us, and so do I.

Please accept this document as official notification of my resignation. I would humbly request that my personal affects be shipped to my residence.

Sincerely,
Jeremy L. Bassett

A DIVINE SENSE OF HUMOR

SAM

Sam hated everybody. Everybody sucked. They were all assholes. He hated each and every person on Earth, including the millions he'd never even met. He hated everyone except for the redheaded girl that sat in front of him in Lit class.

He loved her.

One day, Sam nervously decided to profess his love to the redheaded girl. He went up to her before class and decided to ask her out for a date on Saturday. She looked at him in shock and said, with every ounce of excitement in her, "YES! YES! I've been waiting all year for this."

So, Sam and the redheaded girl went out and they kept going out for several months. Sam became a much happier camper and threw away his twenty-seven pairs of black jeans.

And, after seven months with the redheaded girl, Sam loved everybody. Everybody was great. He loved each and every person on Earth, including the millions he'd never even met. He loved everybody, except for the little redheaded girl.

He hated her now.

TWO WEIRDOES, A SHOVEL,
AND LOTS OF OPEN LAND

John Collins came upon the open field at precisely twelve midnight, not a minute before and not a minute after, but precisely at midnight, and when I say precisely, I do mean precisely. He'd looked at his watch after wiping the sweat from his brow with the sleeve of his white turtleneck. John was thirsty and he was tired, and most of all he was pissed off. Another fight with Connie meant another voyage into the wilderness.

John Collins came upon the open field at precisely twelve midnight, not a minute before and not a minute after, but precisely at midnight, and well, you get the point. Sitting in the middle of the field were two strange looking men, one very tall and the other—well he was, well, pretty normal. It's hard to describe what the other one looked like because well, he kind of looked like everyone else, and trying to describe everyone else would be quite a chore, considering I'm not quite sure who everyone else is.

I bet you thought I was going to begin this paragraph with 'John Collins came upon the open field... blah, blah, fucking blah.' You were wrong. And so was John in thinking that he came upon the open field at twelve midnight exactly. He had forgotten his watch had stopped for but a moment last Thursday during his weekly card game with the guys. And so, he had actually entered the field at 12:00:01 and not 12:00:00 as previously thought.

John Collins came upon the field at 12:00:01 and that is the last time I am going to say that. He saw the two weirdoes sitting there in the middle of all this open land and all they had with them, or so it seemed from as far away as he was, was a large metal shovel.

John Collins walked towards the two weirdoes, his thirst taking over. Maybe they had some water. No matter how odd they looked, he had to try. His throat was counting on him.

As he grew closer, John clenched his fists, readying himself for anything that might come. "Excuse me, you two wouldn't happen to have any—"

The tall one cut him off: "Sit down."

John thought about the command for a second and decided they couldn't be that bad. He needed water and they might have some for him. And so it came to pass that John Collins sat down with the two weirdoes at precisely 12:06:35.

"So, what I was going to ask was—"

The tall one looked over at his rather normal looking companion and spoke. "So, tell me, Joseph, have you ever read the Bible?"

The rather normal-looking fellow, whose name was apparently Joseph, looked up from the campfire to his rather tall comrade. "The Bible, I must've taken a look at it."

The tall one rubbed his chin. "Do you remember the Gospels?"

Joseph smiled at his taller, less normal-looking friend. "I remember the maps of the holy land, colored they were, very pretty. The Dead Sea was this pale blue. The very look of it made me thirsty. 'That's where we'll go,' I used to say. That's where we'll go on our honeymoon. We'll swim and we'll be happy."

Joseph and his giant of a compatriot looked at each other and burst into tears.

John was reminded of the Acting I class he took twenty years ago, the one he had to take seven times to get into Acting II because he just wasn't a good enough performer. He remembered having to memorize this scene a thousand times with a thousand different partners and how everyone at Kimball knew it, but for some godforsaken reason, he could no longer remember the name.

Joseph's taller, freakier-looking friend wiped the tears from his face. "You should've been a poet."

Joseph sniffled, "I was. Isn't that obvious?"

And then it came to John in a flash. He knew. He knew! "*Waiting for Godot*, right?" He screamed with delight through the painful dryness, his voice cracking as it had when he was twelve, going on thirteen.

Both weirdoes' jaws drooped. "No. He already came and went."

John chuckled, "No, I mean that's the play you were reciting. *Waiting for Godot* is the name of the play."

Joseph sneered at John. "Yes. We know that. What do you think we are, stupid or something? And by the way, who invited you to sit down?"

The taller, weirder looking guy said to his shorter, more normal friend, "I did, you freak. This is our new friend Beelzebub."

John arched an eyebrow. "Actually, my name is John."

The tall freak of nature said back, "John, Beelzebub—whatever floats your boat."

The shorter more average looking Joseph told his friend, "Robert, I think this guy is a putz."

The tall one, who apparently was called Robert, slapped his friend in the face. Robert slapped Joseph so hard that Joseph lost his balance and fell backwards off his tree stump and flat onto his ass. "Joseph, that is no way to speak to our guest."

Robert turned to John. "Please forgive my friend Joseph Smart. He is somewhat of an idiot. And, oh bother, where have my manners flittered away to? I have yet to introduce myself." The tall man extended his hand. "My dear Beelzebub, my name is Robert Short."

John shook the hand of his new friend. "My name is really John Collins, not Beelzewhatever, and all I came over for was a—"

Robert cut him off, "A good conversation, right?"

"Well actually," John interjected. "What I came over for was to see if maybe either of you had any—"

"Booze?!" Joseph screamed, crawling back onto his tree stump. "Is that what you came looking for, Beelzebub? Booze?! We are not that kind of people, Mr. Man. We are honest, hard-working, Christian men."

"I think somebody needs a slap," Robert threatened. "You are such a liar, Joe. You haven't been to church once in your entire life."

"How would you know, you jackass?"

"You told me, dickhead!" Robert smacked him again, sending Joseph back to the ground. "Why do you have to be such a prick? We have a guest and if booze is what he wants, don't give him some crock of shit about being a good Christian man. Just give him the booze and leave him be. What'd Beelzebub ever do to you?"

John wanted to speak his disgust with the name they had chosen for him, but his throat was vehemently against it. The only words he could mutter were: "Water, I need water."

"Oh, you want water now?" Joe said as he rose, dusting himself off. "It's always you, you, you. Everybody better please Beelzebub, yest ye be destroyed."

Robert stared at his companion, then at John. "Don't mind Joe. He's a bit obnoxious. Here," Robert said, reaching into the knapsack laying at his feet, and pulling from it a bottle of Evian. "Have some of this. It's supposed to be really good."

John sucked at the bottle, the lukewarm water soothing his throat just enough to ease the pain, but not nearly enough to rid him of it. "Thank you, Robert."

"You're more than welcome. So, what brings you to the wilderness this fine night?"

John looked down, not wanting to remember. He had so enjoyed these past few moments of forgetting about Connie and their argument. "It's my wife, man. She booted me out of the house. Said I was being an asshole for not apologizing to her for something I didn't even do. Said I should go somewhere and figure out why she was mad and not come back till I was prepared to apologize."

"Can't say I blame her. You are an asshole," Joe whispered, ducking prematurely, anticipating a slap from Robert, which did in fact come, but not until two seconds later, when Joe had returned to a normal sitting position and thought he was safe. It was a quick, 'WHAM' and just like that, the back of Rob's hand smacked into Joe's face and the shorter, more ordinary-looking fellow who happened to have quite the attitude fell back unconscious.

"That sounds pretty unfair, Beelzebub. What did you do?" Robert stared at John. "Did you sleep with another woman? Did you sleep with another man? Leave the seat up? Did you make fun of her latest novel?"

"She's not a writer."

"That's not important. What is important is what you did. If I knew that, I could help you."

"I didn't do anything!" John bellowed.

"Well, you obviously did something or you wouldn't be this defensive."

"I didn't do anything!"

"Oh, I know, you fed the dog cat food. Am I right, or am I right?"

"I don't have a dog!" shouted John. "I have a horse, and it got loose because of the damn vet. He was coming to take a look at it and he forgot to close the gate on his way out and my wife thinks it's my fault because I didn't remind the guy to close the gate. My fault?! What kind of idiot forgets to close the door to a horse's stable?"

"Now Beelzebub, calm down and tell me: was it a male horse or a female horse? It's very important that we know."

"What the hell does it matter if it had balls or not?! It fucking got away and probably got hit by a car or something by now, and my wife is pissed off at me and thinks it's my fault! I thought you said you could help me. All you're doing is being an annoying little gnat!"

"I'll chalk that insult up to anxiety, Beelzebub, and forget about it."

"And another thing, my name is John! Not Beelzebub! It's John"

"I think I've discovered your problem, Beelzebub. You're having an identity crisis and your wife can't deal with it. You think your name is John and you lash out at anyone who says otherwise. Beelzebub, you must learn to control your anger."

John stood, sweat beading up on his forehead, his throat screaming for salvation once more. "I'm going!"

"And yet, how is it—this is not boring you, I hope—how is it that of the four evangelists, only one speaks of a thief being saved, they were all there, or thereabouts, but only one speaks of a thief being saved. Come, Gogo, return the ball! Can't you, once in a way?"

"What?" John said in annoyance, looking down at Robert.

"Sorry, merely having a flashback to the time when Joseph and I were waiting for Godot."

"You are positively insane. I don't know why I'm still here. For all I know, you could be an axe-murderer."

"Actually, it was a hatchet if you want to get technical."

John stood silent. He was talking to a murderer, a real life murderer, not some jackass on the Internet calling himself ISHOT2PAC just to piss off the rap community. John couldn't move, until of course he realized, *I could be next!*

"Shit!" he screamed, trying to bolt away from the two weirdoes, held back by the heavy hand of his would-be attacker.

The shadow of Robert came over him. John blabbered: "Oh fuck, oh Jesus, oh my God, I'mgonnadie!" John looked up at the shit-eating grin on his attacker's face. "Please don't kill me." he begged. He felt his bladder release.

"My dear Beelzebub, why would I want to kill you?"

"Why wouldn't you kill me?" John asked, examining the expanding stain on his pants.

"You're my friend, Beelzebub. I want to help you."

The two of them walked back over to the campfire and sat down. John muttered, under his breath, "I can't believe I pissed my pants. I haven't pissed my pants since that time in kindergarten when the teacher's aide wouldn't let me in to use the bathroom during recess."

Robert motioned to the still motionless Joseph. "Don't worry. He does it all the time."

John, completely confused by the absurdity of the situation, sat down. He couldn't escape, so why try? Besides, Rob had said he wasn't going to kill him. Out of curiosity, John asked. "Who did you kill, if you don't mind me asking?"

Robert fumbled through the knapsack again, this time pulling out a package of Hostess chocolate cupcakes. He ripped open the plastic and handed John one. "My wife," he said. "I killed my wife."

John munched away at his cupcake. "What did she do?"

Still working at his cupcake Robert answered, "Shee swepped wid Joseff."

John looked over at the sleeping weirdo. "Joseph?"

Robert brushed the crumbs away from his mouth. "Yeah, Joseph. The bastard. He's been stealing chicks from me since high school. That wasn't quite what happened this time though."

"Do tell," John pushed, finishing off his cupcake.

"You see, me and my wife, and Joe and his wife, we were all really drunk one night. And of course, me and Joe, being men, we were horny, so we were calling out our wives names and they just so happened to be so drunk they both ended up playing hide the salami with the wrong husband."

John gagged on his second cupcake, spitting three chew's worth out onto Robert's lap. "How drunk were they? I mean, were they so drunk they couldn't even remember their names?"

Robert stood up and shook his finger at John. "You see: therein lies the problem, my dear Beelzebub. They both have the same name."

John grinned, not knowing why he found this so funny. "Your wives both have the same name? What is it?"

"Connie."

John's eyes widened and his pulse quickened. "Connie? It's an awful small world. My wife's Connie too."

Joseph reawakened with a start, shooting upright, and locking his gaze on John. Robert stared at John as well, his jaw hung low. "That is your problem, friend."

"What's my problem?" John inquired.

Joseph scowled at him. "Your wife's name, idiot. All women named Connie are evil."

"Now wait a minute, just because the two of you got plastered one night and your wives each ended up riding the wrong hobby horse doesn't mean all Connies are evil. My Connie is far from evil. She's just having a difficult time dealing with the loss of our horse. She's not evil."

"Oh, that's what she'd like you to believe," Robert interjected. "Oh, my dear friend, she is leading you into a trap. All Connies are evil! We learned this the hard way, but you don't have to. You must kill her, Beelzebub. You must rid the world of her evil."

John laughed at them. "You two are the most deranged pair of shitfucks I've ever met. I'm going to kill my wife just because you two say so?"

"You are?!" Robert said. "At last, Joseph, our dear Beelzebub has seen the light."

"So, how are you going to kill her?" Joseph wondered, rubbing his chin as if the star of a 40s detective novel.

This was nuts, but he might as well play along. He stopped giggling and took on a rather serious monotone. "I don't know. Do you have any suggestions?"

"As a matter of fact, I do," Robert said, excitedly reaching into the knapsack one more time, this time pulling out what appeared to be a gun of some sort, a big gun, a big, black gun, a big, black, semiautomatic gun. An Uzi 9mm. "Use this."

John took it and looked at Robert, then back at the gun, then back at the size of the knapsack, realizing how small it was and how this big black gun could never have fit in there. "Where did you get this?"

"Is it convenient?" Joseph queried.

"Yeah, I guess," John answered.

"Then don't ask," Robert added.

"So, can I go now?" John wondered.

"Yes, be off, and don't come back till you have rid the world of that evil beast you call wife," Robert proclaimed, in his sternest impression of Orson Welles.

As he was walking away, Joseph pulled him aside and said to him, "Let me give you just one bit of advice, Beelzebub." They stopped, and Joseph smiled at him. "I thought you were an asshole from the start. Still do. But I can sympathize with you now. I had to kill my wife too. An old friend told me that all

Connies were evil and I didn't believe him till I saw my wife riding a bologna pony that wasn't mine. He also told me that most coke addicts don't make good writers. You remember those two things and you'll get through this. We have faith in you kid."

John smiled and turned away, waving a quick goodbye, before cracking up the entire way home.

As he neared the house, John looked at the gun. On the handle was inscribed the name, "Arnold Friend." He threw it into the bushes, shaking his head.

John ascended the steps of his house; there, on the porch, lay his wife Connie, fast asleep in the swing. He sat down beside her, draping her legs over his own and wondering what this whole night had meant. And then he realized what it meant.

Nothing.

It meant absolutely nothing. In life, sometimes things just happen. He just happened to bump into two weirdoes, a shovel, and lots of open land. It wasn't a life-changing event. It just happened. Some things just happen. He sank back into the seat of the swing and closed his eyes, content with himself.

AND IF YOU'RE wondering what the hell difference it made that John walked onto the field at 12:00:01 and not 12:00:00—well, it didn't make a damn bit of difference at all, but you read the story anyway, didn't you?

THE BREAKDOWN

Joel Pishman tapped his spoon against his water glass and the insane melodrama of the cafeteria quieted. He leaped up onto his chair, standing there with a certain indescribable panache. "Ladies and gentleman," he began, "I just wanted to let you all know your friendly neighborhood literary magazine is sponsoring a campus-wide nervous breakdown in the Student Union tonight. You are all invited, encouraged, and—if necessary —are being told to come to the event. Thanks a bunch!"

He carefully stepped down from his perch and picked up his tray. He was so happy with himself that he couldn't stand it. Joel Pishman had never announced anything in the cafe before. He had always been too shy and had one of his friends do it for him. But today, today Joel Pishman had become a man.

Well, not really. There was still the matter of the girl he liked but was afraid to ask out, and of course the story he had overdue for his Advanced Fiction class, and then he couldn't forget about the literary magazine, of which he was co-chair. The magazine still didn't have any submissions a whole two months into the semester. Yeah, his life sucked. It blew goats. It was a yawning chasm of pain.

But that was everybody else's life nowadays. That was why Joel had organized this whole campus-wide breakdown in the first place, that and the fact that his organization was required to perform some act of community service during the semester. And what better service could he offer to the community?

He was pretty good in bed, but he was a straight male, and straight (or even bisexual) females were pretty hard to come by nowadays. Or to come with, for that matter. This was a campus of lesbians, through and through.

So, Joel Pishman brought his tray up to the nifty little hole in the wall where everyone put their trays to be swallowed up by the kitchen staff. He walked out of the dining hall and made his way through the building till he reached the back door which led to the path, which was coincidentally not paved with yellow brick, which led to the Student Union, which coincidentally, and you'd know this already if you had been paying attention earlier, was the designated site of the campus-wide breakdown that had coincidentally been planned by one Joel Pishman, who coincidentally is the hero of our story, that is if you believe in heroes, coincidentally of course.

Joel pranced up the stairs to the main floor of the Student Union where he hoped his staff awaited him. He hoped, rather than expected, because Joel was a very passive boy. He didn't like to upset people and he didn't like to harass them, though most girls never minded if he harassed them because as I mentioned before, he was particularly good in bed. That aside, Joel pranced into the Student Union, hoping and praying that his staff was already preparing the place for the big event.

He was very disappointed when none of them were anywhere to be found. Well, I guess "very disappointed" is putting it mildly. He was pissed. No, I still find that to be a weak description of his state of mind. How about, 'he was motherfucking pissed'? Yeah, that has a better ring to it. He was motherfucking pissed.

He threw his sorry ass into a chair and began to pout. He was good at pouting. He did it well. It was about the only thing he did do well. Joel couldn't ask the girl out, and the magazine was falling apart. He was failing all his classes and worst of all, he had writer's block, which his Advanced Fiction professor denied the existence of. His life was a piece of shit and he knew it.

"Fuck," he muttered as he tapped his fingers on the table to the rhythm of some song he'd gotten stuck in his head this morning before he'd left for his acting class. "Fuck, fuck, fuck," he continued. "Fuck!" he screamed at the top of his lungs, bringing to him the attention of the entire room. "Sorry," he apologized, waving to all of them. God, his life sucked.

Then, out of nowhere, he heard her voice, that sweet, sexy voice. "Joel," she began, placing her hand on his shoulder. "Are you all right?"

He turned to face her, that beautiful face, those gorgeous eyes.

"Yeah, I'm fine," he informed her. "How are you?"

"I'm good. Listen, I heard about that nervous breakdown you're planning to have up here tonight."

"Kinda silly, huh?"

"Yeah," she giggled. "Well, I've seen stranger things."

He chuckled, admiring her smile. "Like what?"

"Like there was this one time I saw these two guys sitting out in a field with a shovel reciting lines from *Waiting for Godot*. That was pretty weird. I heard that Sam Beckett's lawyers had a field day with them because they screwed up a line."

"That is pretty strange." Joel replied.

"Yeah," she smiled. "But anyway, the real reason I came over here was to see what you were doing on Friday. I was wondering if you'd like to take a trip into Boston with me?"

To say that Joel got a little excited after hearing this would have been akin to saying the bomb the United States dropped on Hiroshima did a 'little' damage.

"You want to go into Boston with me?"

"Yeah sure. Why not? You're a cute guy, and I hear you're good in bed."

He blushed. "Well, I don't like to brag."

She smirked. "So, are we on for Friday?"

He was happy as a schoolgirl. "Yes."

She smiled, gave him a peck on the cheek, and walked away. Maybe his life wasn't a yawning chasm of pain after all.

❧

IT HAD BEEN an hour and no one had shown up yet, but the incident with the girl still fresh in his mind, Joel sat patiently, contently, awaiting his staff. After waiting for about an hour, five minutes, and forty-point-six seconds, Joel was joined by his illustrious literary magazine staff.

"Sorry we're late," the first one muttered, trying desperately to catch his breath. "We just got done sorting through a whole shitload of submissions."

"Submissions?" Joel questioned, his mind still fixed on the image of the girl's smile.

"Yeah, boss," the second one began to explain. "Submissions for the magazine. You know, the one you're in charge of?"

Joel's eyes lit up. "You mean we've got submissions."

The first one had an ear to ear grin. "Yup. Guess the magazine isn't going to be a bust, after all."

Joel sank back in his chair and smiled, happier than a schoolgirl. "That's great! Now get to work all of you. There's going to be a breakdown in here any minute."

❧

JOEL WATCHED as his lackeys decorated the Student Union and prepared it for the massive nervous breakdown he'd helped to organize. The trouble was he wasn't so sure he was going to have a breakdown anymore. Two of his major problems had just been solved. Now all he had to worry about were his poor grades and his writer's block.

About the time he finished that thought, a woman came running in. "Joel!" she screamed. "Joel!" she bellowed. "Joel! Oh, there you are. I've got terrible news. Your roommate has just died."

His jaw dropped. He didn't like his roommate anyway, so it didn't really bother him. "That's horrible."

"I know," she said, wrapping her arms around him. "I didn't really think you should have to deal with this on top of everything else, but someone had to tell you. I'm so sorry. But look at the bright side: At least now you've got an automatic 4.0. College policy says so."

His roommate was dead, and he was grinning from ear to ear. He might as well have been a schoolgirl.

❧

WELL, now Joel was a bit confused. He had nothing to have a nervous breakdown about. His life was perfect. He had the girl. He had the magazine. He had a 4.0. He was sure the writer's block was only temporary. Shit, he was thinking of calling the whole thing off. Unfortunately for him about two hundred stressed-out college students had already shown up.

He stepped up to the microphone to begin the event at precisely twelve midnight not a minute before, and not a minute after, but precisely at midnight, and when I say precisely, I do mean precisely. He tapped it to make sure it was on and it let out a monstrous cry of feedback. "Hello, everyone."

"Hello, Joel," they replied in unison.

"Welcome to the First Annual Campuswide Nervous Breakdown. For those of you who may not know, I am Joel Pishman, co-chair of your friendly neighborhood literary magazine and—Shit! I can't do this. I'm not depressed enough. Somebody else should come up here, cause I simply cannot have a nervous breakdown tonight."

The crowd was suddenly and coincidentally restless. "What do you mean?" one of them shouted out to him. "You have to have a breakdown, Joel."

"I don't need to anymore. My life has gotten better."

"But none of us know how to have a breakdown, Joel. You have to show us."

"I thought you already said you were having a breakdown. Why do you need my help?" Joel pondered.

"Well, y'know, sometimes people say things they don't mean, Joel."

"Are you getting all existential on me?"

"That's not fucking existentialism, dipshit. Fucking Sartre—now, that's fucking existentialism. All that shit about the body and the mind..." The boy trailed off, his eyes glossing over, his jaw drooping, his train of thought lost round a bend. Then, suddenly, with newfound fury, he shouted, "Why can't you have a fucking breakdown like the rest of us?!"

"I'm simply not upset anymore."

"You're a dickhead."

"Come on."

"You dragged us all here under the impression that we were going to have one massive, collective, nervous breakdown. And now here you are, ruining the whole fucking thing."

"How am I ruining it? You can still have the breakdown. There's still a couple hundred people here."

"That's not my fucking point, Joel. You are missing the fucking point. Either all of us have a breakdown, or none of us do. That's the way it works."

"That's absurd."

"Joel, you're absurd. I'm absurd. We're all fucking absurd. Normal people don't like us. That's why we all came to this school. That's why we all came to this event. If we don't stick together we get shit on by the normals. They divide and they conquer Joel. That's how they work. So, to protect ourselves, we all gotta be absurd, or we all gotta be normal. And we sure as hell don't wanna be normal, Joel. Do you know what that means?"

"What does it mean?" Joel queried, wiping the sweat from his brow.

"That means, either you have to kill us, which for some reason I don't see happening, no matter how many girls you seduce cause you're good in bed. Or, we kill you, which I find to be the easier, more sensible option."

"You're gonna kill me?"

"Yup."

"Oh well. I guess I had it coming."

"Don't even try it, Joel. Don't try to be absurd now. We're still going to kill you."

"Why?! For God's sake, why?"

"Because it's a rule, Joel. In stories written in college creative writing classes, someone always dies."

"But if someone always dies, wouldn't it be more absurd to let me live?"

The crowd laughed and its spokesman began again. "Therein lies the absurdity, Joel. Therein lies the absurdity."

They were rushing the stage as he breathed his final words: "Where does it lie? Where does it lie?"

JOEL PISHMAN WAS FOUND HANGING from the rafters of the Student Union several hours later. The coroner later deduced it was a fast death and that his neck had snapped almost instantly.

There was a note attached to his body: "Joel, thanks for the breakdown."

The campus safety officers made a note to remind the Office of Campus Activities that the literary magazine had completed its community service.

A RIVER RUNS THROUGH THESE
THREE POINTS OF VIEW

Jacob laid the body at the banks of the tiny green river that ran behind his house. He looked down at the body, the body of his pool cleaner. Bob. He had never been close to any of the workers. They were like ghosts in the house. No one was to speak with them or ever acknowledge their existence unless they screwed something up. Bob was different though. First of all, Bob was a good fuck.

Jacob had been sleeping with Bob since that night by the pool when Jacob noticed how cute Bob's ass was, how round it was, and how snug it fit into his jean cut-offs. Now that hot ass was lying in the cold mud, dead.

Bob had hung himself after losing his job. Jacob's father found the two of them in bed and ordered Bob out of the house immediately. Jacob looked down at his lost love and cried, wondering how his father could do this to them.

The river was his only hope now. His mother had told him stories about the magical river when he was a boy. She had told him that once, long ago, a princess had brought her dying prince to the river's banks and placed him into the waters, instantly reviving him.

He'd always thought the story bullshit, a product of his mother's nightly martini binge, but he had to try something.

Jacob slowly pushed Bob's body into the water. He waited for the glow that his mother had always so vividly described, but no glow came. Instead, the body began to float downstream.

Jacob ran into the river, his hands flailing, splashing him with water and muck. He reached for the body but stopped at the sound of a bellow from behind.

"Freeze, asshole!" the man in blue screamed. "You're under arrest."

2.

I hate canoeing. I hate canoeing.

"Gabe," my father asked, "Enjoying the trip?"

"Oh yeah, Dad." I proclaimed in my best impression of a happy camper.

"I love canoeing," said Dad.

I HATE CANOEING! I hate the smell of my father, who never showers before we go out on one of these little adventures. I hate the stench of the water and the mosquitoes. The smell of the bait I don't mind much, but God do I hate the fucking mosquitoes. Being away from my computer for so long is hell. I hate the outdoors.

"Isn't it wonderful to be outside for a change, son?"

"Yeah, I love the air. It's so fresh."

I'll tell you what's fresh. The Fresh Prince. He's fucking fresh. And I'd be watching the fucking marathon on the WB right now if I wasn't here rowing this fucking sack of shit, watching the water rush by, the cool blue-green, and the body—

"Oh my God, Dad, it's a body!"

My dad, half-drunk from his first three brews, looked at it and said, "Nonsense. It's just an alligator."

"There aren't any alligators in Maine!"

Dad shrugged.

I continued to row, a little harder now.

I hate canoeing.

3.

Bob, by this time, was at the end of the river, and by this time he was waking up. He had a terrible headache and his ass was sore. He remembered that he hadn't pulled the butt-plug out before hanging himself.

"I HUNG MYSELF?" he screeched.

What the fuck was he doing alive? As he rose from the river, he felt the heat of a thousand flashbulbs of flickering off at him. Cops, newspaper people, they were all around. How had they gotten here so fast? Why were they all here?

"We'll pay one mill for your story!"

"Will you talk to us?"

"Will you fuck me?"

"Don't fuck her. She doesn't deserve that big hog of yours. Fuck me!"

He looked down and saw his thick phallus flapping in the wind. It was only then that he realized he wasn't wearing any pants.

GOD

THE FINE ART OF LETTING GO

A s the lights dimmed, the crowd's dull roar grew to an untamed wall of sound. The band took the stage. I was lagging behind as I always did, trying to make my entrance count. Staring out at the throng, I wondered what they were all about. How many were fifteen-year-old girls getting trampled in the pit because of their crush on me? How many were forty-year-old men grasping onto the last vestiges of their youth, trying not to notice they were losing their hair? I wondered if anybody gave a damn what the music and the words were about anymore. It was all about the image now, the "dark industrial band" visage the record company had created for us. It didn't matter what I was singing. We could have played Barry Manilow covers.

Boris took to the drums and threw himself into the opening march of "Divine Hatred," our latest single. The lights pulsed, following the lead of his toms, and smoke from the dry ice filled the stage. I ran my fingers through my hair, pushed it back from my face, and gave myself a "fuck it" speech, orating to the voices in my head. I stepped out into the light, vinyl pants, leather jacket, and all.

❧

I STEPPED out into the light as I had every night for the past year, but this time it was different. I never wanted to believe the bullshit about a great white light and no turning back. When I was six, Dad fed me a line. "It's glorious moment son, like being born again." My father was full of Catholic bullshit. I was there when the cancer took my mother and he wasn't. She screamed her fucking lungs out. It wasn't a glorious moment. There was no God, no savior. Wouldn't he have spared her the pain?

Trouble was, I met God when I stepped into the light for the last time. It was a pretty humbling experience. I'd pompously named myself Johnny Baptist and gone on tour to convert the masses, to Atheism that is. I'd earned my money singing God was dead only to end up on the other side and be proved quite wrong.

❧

AFTER THE CONCERT, I didn't go back to my hotel. My manager had pleaded with me, but I was fucked up and not listening. Two days prior, in New York, I had slept with my ex. I wanted us back together but she couldn't deal with the heroin. *Good for her*, I'm thinking now, but at that point my head was still a mess. I had to get out.

In Boston that last night, I took a trip to the old apartment in the Back Bay and caught up with an old friend who still lived in the building. He could tell I was jonesing and he helped me out. We shot up on his living room floor and stared at a hand-made Indian tapestry he'd hung. After five minutes, I took off with the rest. My heart gave out on me on the front steps. It was strong shit. The last thing I remember is my old landlady holding my head in her lap, stroking my hair while someone called 911 on their cell-phone.

I STOOD in front of Him, wondering if He'd let me in for a quick chuckle before throwing me into the Pit personally for all the belittling I had done.

"Why do you insist on wearing those awful pants?" He asked.

"You brought me here to rap about my fashion sense?"

"It was just a question, Johnny."

"Why did you bring me here?"

He chuckled, "I did not bring you, Johnny. I do not have the authority. You do. You choose Heaven or Hell, not I."

"Do you speak English?"

He smiled, "What I was trying to say, in layman's terms is: You can give yourself Hell, or you can make your life Heaven. It is all up to you. That is why you have minds of your own. It distresses me so few of you use them."

"You don't think you should help us out a bit?"

"I am a kind father. Only Ten Commandments have I made, and along with them a lenient eighty- to ninety-year curfew. What you do with it all is up to you."

I half-smirked at the Holy Wiseass. "So you're saying I could be a mass murderer, and as long as I loved it, I would end up in heaven?"

"In a manner of speaking, yes. You would not end up in my heaven, because I set down rules, among which are the words, 'thou shalt not kill,' but Heaven, Hell, life, death—it is all just a matter of perception. One man's treasure is—"

"Another man's trash," I finished. God spoke in clichés, but if it all started with him were they really clichés when he spoke them?

"How is my heaven different?" I asked him. "Which is better, and why am I here? Are you trying to say that my heaven is the same as yours?"

"Well, as I said, it is all a matter of perception. One man's heaven is no less special than another's." He rubbed His graying beard. "And no, your heaven is not the same as mine, not exactly... but they are similar enough that I saw fit to bring you here."

"Bring me here? You said you had no control over my afterlife."

"You suffered much in your time on Earth. I sought merely to reward you."

"But how would you know what my heaven is? How would you know?"

"I am your father. I know all."

"A common misconception among parents. If you know all, why don't you use that knowledge to help your people? Why do you leave them to rot and reward me?"

"You are special, Johnny."

"I was a fucking heroin addict, singing songs that proclaimed you and your faith dead. How am I more special than that old landlady of mine who's been devoted to you her entire life and is stuck running a crowded apartment building for the rest of her days?"

"A long time ago, Johnny, I made a mistake. I thought I could trust my children, and so I let them loose on Earth. I gave them one rule for eternal happiness and they could not follow it. They chose to suffer."

"Sure. *They* chose. But does that mean you have the right to condemn the rest of us for the rest of our days, punish the many for the sins of the one, and reward only the few? Do one woman's mistakes give you the right to screw us over for all eternity?"

"There was a perfection in that garden, Johnny, but they wanted more freedom. They wanted a life without rules and that was, what would you call it, a pipe-dream."

"Are you saying that subservience is the only way to perfection?"

"The mind, the gift she asked for—subconsciously or not—when she ate that apple, comes with a price. Thinking is not perfect. Free will is the opportunity to, as you say, 'screw up,' to do whatever it is you want to do. You cannot expect there to not be a cost. That is not logical."

"Then why not give us all the chance for perfection? Why not—"

"Would you truly prefer to be mindless?" He asked, sinking back into His recliner, His white hair falling and framing His face, the glow of His eyes, the sharp angles of His jaw, and the intricate wrinkles that ran across His forehead.

"No I wouldn't, but what about senseless violence? What about babies dying? Car accidents? Plane crashes? Terrorism? What of all that senseless bullshit? That stuff is all pretty mindless."

"All bad decisions on someone's part."

"So you're willing to sit back and watch innocent kids die because some guy drank a little too much Jack and rammed his fucking car into a nursery school?"

"I am not perfect."

"Why not?"

"I chose free will a long time ago too, Johnny. I can make bad decisions just as easily as you."

"Well, why not correct them? Why not fix your mistakes?"

"Sometimes a father just has to let go."

"Let go? The Holocaust, was that letting go? How about two world wars, and countless others—were they letting go? I somehow think you just aren't taking responsibility for your children."

"I cannot wipe your bottoms forever, Johnny. There comes a time when you have to learn to take care of yourselves. I am not this almighty, all-powerful being your so-called prophets make me out to be. I am one man, albeit, a very powerful one; very simply, I am a father. I have not a bit more power than your father did. It has taken me a long time, but I have learned the fine art of letting go."

With my thumb and index finger I rubbed and then pinched the bridge of my nose.

"Do you understand?"

"I think you're asking a lot. I didn't even believe you existed ten minutes ago."

He pulled His long white hair out of His face and cracked a small smile, "Well, Johnny, is there anything you would like to know?"

"You know, you're a much nicer guy than I thought you would be."

"You atheists are getting the wrong picture of me down there. It is the so-called religions, making up names for me, trying to convince people that their theory is right. I guess I have no one to blame but myself. I did create you, after all. I just assumed you would use your minds to think for yourselves rather than to try and concoct ludicrous stories about floods and parting seas, and aliens and thetans. Communities are all well and good, so long as individuality is not lost. That is what those religions are all about, making everyone believe the same thing. That is why I never come to visit anymore, so to speak. I am sick of all the politics. I am sick of it all."

"Why not just destroy it?" I questioned.

"A father could never destroy his children so easily. They may annoy me to no end, but they are still the fruits of long hours of creation, and though they may spend their entire lives devoted to some ridiculous notion that God can be reached only by getting on their knees, I still love them."

"How does that work?"

"Creation?"

I nodded.

"You did not have sexual education in high school?

"You have a wife or something?"

"It is strictly an act of the mind. Well, I guess it is more complex than that, but I do not like to brag."

Twenty-seven years of finely honed cynicism were melting away like margarine in a frying pan. "Go ahead and brag. I've got all of eternity, right?"

He laughed. "Johnny, I knew there was a reason Peter sent you to me. He makes all of my appointments you know, sort of a secretary. Or what is it you call them nowadays, an 'administrative assistant.' Yes, that's it. Only schedules the interesting individuals. Office politics you know? I do not like them much more than the politics down below, but you have to have some kind of organization, do you not?"

I'm an interesting person? To God?

"Johnny," He said.

"Yeah. Yeah I guess you do have to have some kind of organization."

My feet were tired and it felt awkward standing while He sat. The floor looked mighty good. "Do you mind if I sit?"

"Of course not. Make yourself comfortable."

I sat Indian-style on the floor. It chilled me through the vinyl pants and reminded me that I was sans-underwear. I hoped He hadn't noticed.

"I'd been meaning to ask you," I began nervously, "What do you think of my music?"

"Why, Johnny," He smiled, "That is a whole other story."

❦ III ❧
THE FALLEN ANGELS OF
KIMBALL COLLEGE

DEATH BY CURSOR

The gold numbers 416 hung on a modest wooden door with a single lock. It was swung half-open, the entrance secured only by a strip of yellow police tape. Despite what my parents and high school friends had told me, you actually didn't need more than a solitary lock in Lowell on most nights. It wasn't the cesspool us snotty Chelmsford residents had always imagined. Naysayers might simply reply, "It's just that part of Lowell that's nice, and it's because it's the part on the Chelmsford border that it's actually livable." And they might be right, but I have never been a big believer in 'the wrong side of the tracks,' or any other cliché for that matter.

And that's strange, I guess, I thought to myself as Randall and I ducked under the tape that roped off the doorway, as Randall groaned about his bad knees and his bad back, when really it was the size of his Budweiser belly that was to blame for his pain. That was a cliché, wasn't it? Good cop, fat cop, y'know?

That is what it must seem like from the outside, the surface. Probably why most guys head to the academy. It's all so simple: You're the good guy and the other guy, the one with the gun, or the car doing 80 in a 55, he's the bad guy. But most police work is a bit more complex than the crap they air on Fox. *COPS* and *World's Greatest Police Chases IV*—that shit pisses me off.

This particular situation was different, this particular studio apartment with its minimalist furnishings: a flimsy Wal-Mart bookcase and dining set; a hand-me-down cobalt blue pullout couch; and a grungy fish tank with yellow-green water and no fish. There were only two things anywhere near valuable here: a five-year-old Hewlett Packard PC, and what two years ago might have been considered a top of the line entertainment center. This apartment was different. Complicated.

It had been a year since I'd set foot in Apartment 416, and as bad as I'd left things, I'd never expected to return like this.

Randall was huffing and puffing his way through a routine check of the kitchenette area. The four flights of stairs had had their way with my rotund friend. As he did his thing, dusting for prints and such, I made my way to the computer.

I stared at the monitor, at the tedious flashing of the blinking cursor. *That's death.* I thought to myself. *To guys like Marcus Gold, the tenant of Apartment 416, a blinking cursor on a blank page might as well be a bullet in the head.*

This little corner of the apartment was where he wrote. His computer was heaped onto a tiny desk: CPU, monitor, printer, and all the cables that held them together. A computer was so easy to repair. If only human beings were that simple. If only you could go out and replace the defective chip for a couple hundred bucks, or buy a new cable at Circuit City for nineteen ninety-five. Then maybe... Who the hell knows?

The walls that adjoined to form Mark's writing corner were plastered with minuscule letters. They couldn't even dignify him with a full page. Carefully typed, with crisp photocopied signatures, they were no bigger than an index card. It was hard to tell what this was all about without getting in closer. When you got closer, it became the most depressing thing you'd ever seen. They were rejection letters, hundreds of them, plastered to the wall so thick there might not have been any wallpaper underneath. There were thousands of harsh 'no thank yous,' and cold 'not quite it, better luck next times,' and of course there were plenty of the old standby, "Not suitable for our publication. Please try again." This was the backdrop against which Marcus Gold worked each and every day.

༜

I REMEMBERED the day I watched him work a year before. I'd pulled a chair across the room and put my arm around him. He gave me a look and glanced over my nakedness as if he were expecting the badge to be tattooed on my chest, still not used to the whole thing.

"It's like the Village People," he told me.

"How so?" I asked.

"You're the cop, and I'm—"

"The Jew? I don't think there was a Jew." My hands moved to his shoulders, rubbing them gently.

"I'm not Jewish."

"Sorry. Figured with the last name." I stopped my words and my hands, not sure if I should continue.

"Gold?"

"Gold does sound Jewish."

"Catholic." He fidgeted, rolling his shoulders backwards and forwards, signaling me.

I began again. "You're full of surprises."

"I'm the Indian." He typed another word and stopped, looking it over. His shoulders tensed despite some of my best work. The word wasn't right. He hadn't figured out what was wrong with it yet, but he was sure it wasn't right.

"The Indian? How's that?" I read over his shoulder. The word was 'quietly.' *She died quietly*. What was wrong with that? He back-spaced until the offending word was gone. He stared for a moment, silent. Then he deleted the whole sentence, leaving only the blinking cursor on the blank screen again. The best masseuse in the Bay State couldn't pull the tension away now.

"Great-great-grandmother messed around a bit."

"Really?"

"Really." He re-typed the sentence verbatim. He examined it again, and the tension in the pit of his shoulders moved along. He was smiling. He paused. He paused and took a sip of coffee.

"You know he's not the only gay cop in the world."

Putting his mug down, he said, "The guy from the Village People?"

"Yeah."

"Sure he is."

I stopped again, a bit dumbfounded.

"Now, stop talking or else I'm never going to get anything done."

I eyed the wall. There weren't as many back then, but it was still ominous.

"That's better," he said, beginning to type again.

I looked around the floor for my pants. "Why do you keep those letters?"

"Inspiration."

"They inspire you?"

"They remind me."

"Remind you of what?" I paused, pulling the sweat-stained pajama bottoms on. "They would just depress me."

"Which is why you're the cop and I'm the Indian."

"No wonder he killed himself," Randall observed, pulling me back from the bittersweet of my memory and leaving a decidedly more pungent taste in my mouth. Mark wasn't there anymore, just the blinking cursor and the letters on the wall.

I couldn't even look back at Randall. Five years in homicide could turn even Mr. Mom into an unsympathetic fuck. Randall was no exception, but he wasn't that nice to begin with. He was a revolting, fat shit of a cop. I had never been attracted to someone that filthy and I've probably become infatuated with Randall these past few weeks for a change of pace. Mark was anal in more ways than one. He always looked prim and proper. Randall can barely dress himself.

Randall was munching on a blueberry crumb donut. Based solely on the size of his gut, one might guess that blueberry crumb donuts were one of his three basic food groups, right next to Budweiser and Marlboro.

"The first word out of his sister's mouth when I called was 'asshole.' Can you believe that?" Randall licked his fingers clean one by one, probably one of the more disgusting noises ever heard by man.

I continued to scan the wall as I spoke. "Lots of people think you're an asshole, Randall. Just not everybody says it."

I felt the push of his pudgy fist against my shoulder. "Funny. Stanley, she was talking about her brother, this Mark kid. Apparently the whole family thinks he's an asshole and—"

"No wonder he killed himself," I responded, anticipating his snide remark.

"My point exactly, buddy. Nobody liked the guy. Why bother living if nobody can stand you?"

"Very Willy Loman."

"Very who?"

"Willy Loman." I paused, not wanting to believe my partner was that far removed from the real world. "Willy Loman? *Death of a Salesman?*" I gazed into his eyes. Nothing. "It was required reading at most high schools."

"Never heard of it. Must've slept through it."

"This guy Willy Loman ends up killing himself because his definition of success is all about how 'well liked' he is."

"Yeah. Yeah I get you." Randall picked a crumb off his sleeve and ate it. "So, we done?"

I crossed to the living room table. I guess it's ridiculous to call it a living room table. There wasn't really a living room. What little living room there was sat opposite the computer station. It was just the couch and the table, both facing away from the computer and towards the TV. It was his escape, our escape for those two weeks. The speakers were large enough to keep everything else away and the screen on the television set was so immense it could bake a couch potato in ten seconds. This was where he made his final escape. Only a plastic sheet hid the evidence. I retrieved the videotape from the living room table, looked it over for a second, and then held it up for Randall to see. He sighed and shook his head.

"I want to watch it, Randall."

"Again?"

"Yes."

"Here?"

I nodded.

"You mind if I wait in the car, Stan? I think I got another donut down there." He walked towards the door, paused, and then looked back. "You need to do this?"

If he wasn't married, I swear Randall would've been after me in a heartbeat. He was cute when he got all motherly.

I nodded. Yes, I did need to do it.

"I'll be in the car."

Randall closed the door behind him, but the sound and the scent of him lingered for another moment or so. I'm rough on him, but the truth is he really does constantly need a shower.

I inserted the tape into the VCR and turned the television on as I heard Randall's weight descending the stairs. As I sat, the painful rubbing sound of the plastic covering the couch aggravated my headache.

How did I meet Mark? He was arrested for arson and a possible homicide a little less than two years ago. Randall and I had been called in to investigate. Mark had just gotten into a fight with his lover, a transvestite Chinese food delivery boy named Andy. He didn't dress drag when working, Mark assured me.

Andy had gotten pissed at Mark for having a one-night stand with one of his old high school boyfriends. That's why Mark had burned the house down: because Andy had broken up with him. Randall made some comment about how he was a flamer in more ways than one and I sent him for coffee to avoid beating the living shit out of him.

While paperwork and firemen and relatives with angry verbal assaults flew by, I sat and worked it all out with Mark, getting to know him and his side of the story. Some cops didn't bother with that shit. They threw the perp in the back seat and pretended he wasn't there. It was the silent treatment, very high school, but that was the highest level of education some of the guys had achieved, so I couldn't blame them. I liked to talk to the criminals, the vagrants. It kept things interesting.

He didn't talk. Most offenders were so full of shit that it came pouring out straight away, but he didn't talk for a long time. He just sat there looking around, spent thirty seconds staring one direction then moved his head and spent fifteen looking somewhere else.

"Family doesn't like me much," were his first words, about as audible as a lab rat's squeak, and as clear as a pig's grunt.

"Why's that?"

Silence.

"You don't want to tell me?"

"You wouldn't understand. All right?" He shook his head.

"Try me."

Under his breath, he sighed. "Nobody understands."

"You sound like a fourteen-year-old."

"Nobody understands! You don't understand that. You can't. You don't know where I'm coming from."

"Nobody does, do they?"

He looked up and away from me, up into the night sky.

"Nobody understands?" I queried.

He looked off to the side, examining the cruiser, his eyes exploring every twist and curve, every nook and cranny. He didn't want to look at me.

"I can't believe I'm talking to you."

He turned and faced the squad car, counting the dings, the scratches, trying to disturb me with how weird he was. He figured most cops would give up, that most were too dumb to realize what he was doing.

"You need someone to talk to. You need someone who understands."

"What makes you think it's going to be you?" He looked at me dead in the eye.

"I know about bad families."

"Mine takes the fucking cake."

I leaned towards him just a bit to let him know I was interested. "Bet it does."

The list of traumas he'd endured was longer than a spoiled child's Christmas list. His parents had nearly disowned him when he admitted to having a high school affair with Larry Cant. Mark supposed they would have taken it a bit better if Larry hadn't gone on to become a porn star. It was bad enough that a good Catholic boy had reduced himself to sodomy, but to have gone down on one of the most famous cocks in America, that elicited the kind of pissed-off response reserved for an ex flower child just coming down from their last trip to meet their twenty-two-year-old yuppie, suit-wearing motherfucker of a kid for the first time.

His sister almost never called him. She was off living her own lie, so afraid of coming out to her parents after what happened to

Mark that she was close to marrying a pathetic little whelp she'd met just to keep up appearances. Mark had been very vocal in his disapproval of her lying to herself like that. He was very vocal all of the time, liked to use his mouth. That's what got him his nickname: Asshole.

"Val called me asshole once and it stuck. Cute little nickname for Marky the queer. I was never afraid of telling my parents shit. Never. Val, totally different story. So afraid. So indebted. Daddy's little girl. I got by on my own. Didn't owe them anything."

"You weren't afraid."

"They had nothing to hold over my head. It's not like I despised them or anything. I just wasn't about to kiss their ass. They gave me an all right life, till I told them I had a crush on one of Val's boyfriends... Anyway, I told Val she should tell them, that I was really fed up with her living a lie with this guy just to win their approval, and besides, I was great friends with Janet, that's her lover... She didn't understand what I was saying when I told her that the guy was an unimaginative prick, that she could, and was doing better elsewhere."

I nodded.

"Nobody ever really understands the people who speak up." He stared up and off at the sky again.

When we'd finally gotten through all of that, Mark started to talk about the rest of his life, what he was doing now. He'd been writing since he was a kid. It had always been his dream, sort of like me deciding I wanted to be a cop after watching Ponch on *CHiPS* that first time. We'd both held onto our boyhood aspirations. He'd never been published and had enough rejection letters to put out a collection of them, but lots of other people found his writing fantastic—sometimes angsty, but generally fantastic. Even his parents agreed the asshole could write.

The conversation could only last so long. Mark was being hauled off to the slammer, where he would be slammed by half the population. Willing victims were few and far between, after all.

He would get off pretty easily if he behaved. There were no deaths, after all. Maybe we'd get together I told him.

"You a fudgepacker?" he asked me.

"Fudgepacker?" I'm sure the look on my face showed I was pretty disgusted.

"Hey, we queers are allowed to call ourselves whatever we want. So are you?"

"I moonlight."

"Maybe we will get together." He smirked as I loaded him into the car.

"Maybe."

۞

HE GOT OUT A YEAR LATER. I gave him a call that night and we got together at his apartment. I don't think I went home more than twice over those next two weeks. Randall kept noticing how much I was smiling each day, kept asking who the girl was.

"You wouldn't know her," I told him.

Two weeks and it was over. It couldn't have lasted longer. It was like a fever dream, fast and blurry. It's hard to recall any of the details, except that I was happier than I'd ever been, happier than I've been since.

I knew it wouldn't last. I knew that the loner couldn't stand company for long. I also found that the loner needed to go out and show off, and since I wasn't willing to show off, it was bound to cause some problems.

The breakup wasn't as messy as some. It was a simple argument. There was no arson, no loud screaming match. It ended with an agreement that we would both be better off. Knowing it was coming, I took it all right. He was a little worse, a little more broken by yet another rejection.

That's where the tape came in. We'd been apart a little less than a year when the bullet invaded his consciousness. He'd met this guy in prison, a writer who had this thing he did with rejection letters. Each day, for every one he received, he loaded one bullet in a gun, and when the day was over he'd play Russian roulette with his little boy. He blamed his son for why he wasn't writing as well. The kid was eighteen months old, not old enough to know what the hell was going on. The guy said he'd had to sacrifice his dream for his family. Well, one day he got a few too many letters and the gun went off, a bullet ridding him of the dam in his river of dreams, and of the fruit of his loins. He was in jail after serving about a year and a half in a padded room.

Mark liked the idea. Not the kid part. He thought that was crazy. Besides, he was way too involved in himself to consider inflicting pain on someone else.

He got his sister to buy him a gun because he was on probation. He said it was for protection, and I guess it was in a manner of speaking. It was a way of protecting himself from the hurt, the hurt I had caused him, the hurt we had all caused him, the hurt he had hidden in his anger so successfully for so long.

Asshole.

Every day since we'd broken up, he'd done the same thing that the psycho had. He loaded one bullet in the gun for every letter he got, put the gun to his head, and tempted fate. The highest he ever got was four. He was sweating like a pig that day, until the empty chamber fired nothing more than a click of relief.

Mark was a fairly prolific writer and that made this an almost daily ritual. He bought a video camera to tape the ordeal. The tape related the event as if it were as regular a part of his day as brushing his teeth or masturbating his lust away. Get up. Brush teeth. Jerk off. Shower. Get the mail. Load the gun. Pull the trigger. Eat lunch. Write. Sleep.

Nine months later, he finally got what he was looking for: understanding. He got understanding in the form of a bullet in the head. The gun understood the fates; I don't know. God. Maybe, if there is a God, He finally understood.

Mark never thought it would happen. That was on the tape, too. He'd said it just a few moments before pulling the trigger that one last time. Those words were reflected in the crimson puddles that ran across the couch, the abstract designs that played out on the walls.

I caught myself crying. It wasn't a ridiculous sort of crying. It wasn't intense. It was almost obligatory.

The tape stopped and rewound. I rose and collected myself, looking around at the apartment. The emptiness was overwhelming. It was already seeping into every corner of this place, into every crevice. I tried to stay afloat in the silence and my thoughts for a few more moments, contemplating. The loud click of the tape ejecting ended my introspection. I collected the cassette and its case and pulled on my trench coat, shielding my eyes with the dark shades that rested in the right inside pocket.

Writers always had to be so Goddamn tragic, or else they had nothing to write about.

⚜

"I DON'T UNDERSTAND why you get so upset about this shit." I said, holding one of them in my hand. "Its just one person in an office. They aren't the fucking world."

"Yeah. Maybe not. But if they don't like it, the world never fucking sees it."

"That's all that matters?"

"You don't know thing one about the fucking written word, Stanley."

"Just like Loman."

With disbelief, "Willy Loman?"

"Practically required reading at my high school."

"Being well-liked is not the only thing I want, Stanley."

"Sure it is. Understanding. That's what you've wanted since the day I met you. I've tried Mark. I've tried to understand."

"The fuck you have. All you ever do is complain about how upset I get when a letter arrives."

"Cause you base your whole life on what someone else thinks of you."

"Hey, if I owned a fucking printing press, maybe none of this would matter."

"No. You'd just find someone else who hated you and be miserable about that. You need the whole world to love you. You'll never be fucking content with just me."

"No, I won't."

There was a long silence and a cold stare, and then, finally, a slammed door.

I DUCKED under the tape to leave and to my surprise found someone there.

"Who are you?" I queried.

The kid looked at me as if I had three heads. I surveyed him and finally saw the crystal clear brown and gold symbol that should have been a telltale sign.

"UPS?" I responded.

"You're quick," the kid retorted. "I have a package for you."

"For me?"

"Well, for the guy who lives here. But I assume, with the tape and all, it goes to you guys instead."

"How'd you know I was a—"

"You're wearing a badge." The young man asked as I signed: "You a little disoriented, officer?"

"Guess so."

He handed me the package and took flight down the stairs. I unwrapped the parcel slowly and pulled free its contents. The spring issue of the *Northern Nebraska Review* was inside. It looked like someone had gone down to the 7-Eleven, made a few copies, and stapled them together. There was a letter too, a full sheet of eight and a half by eleven, a congratulations. Understanding.

And tears.

"I guess they still can make tragedies like they used to," I said to myself, carrying with me the weight of the tape, the magazine, and the letter. Down the stairs I crept, then out into the cruelty of the January wind.

OUT OF THE GROOVE

Katie fought the jeans all the way up her legs and as the battle roared ever closer to her thighs it seemed as if she might lose the war that day. It wasn't a weight thing. She wasn't fat. Hell, she wasn't even mildly out of shape. Forty-five minutes on her Bowflex, three days a week, plus a half-hour run through the streets of South Berwick the other four days made sure of that. No, the shiny black jeans were meant to be squeezed into. That was part of the look. Like a corset her grandmother would have worn, Katie's jeans were a necessity for a proper night out. The attention they brought was well worth the pain.

The jeans were actually an anomaly in Katie's closet. They stuck out amongst the overalls and the faded Levis, each with their own distinctive holes in the knees. The jeans stood out as if perhaps part of some Halloween costume. Maybe it was the outfit she'd worn to play the part of the club slut at the town's masquerade ball. Or maybe it was reserved for nights when her beau had been extra good and deserved a night of her being extra bad.

Except she didn't have a beau. She hadn't had herself a man in a very long time. A *very* long time.

She'd flipped through all the tops in her closet with no luck. Katie peered into the treacherous ocean of faded T-shirts and had no idea where the other half of this ensemble was. The town's lack of a cultural hot spot was why this outfit hadn't seen the light of day in so long. Since her car's brutal murder at the hands of a March Nor'easter that shut down most of Maine for a week, her travel had been limited to the places her broken down Schwinn 10-speed could take her. Life in sleepy South Berwick didn't require shiny black jeans.

Her sister's knock was the only thing to rescue her from an evening paralyzed by the abyss of her closet. Katie grabbed a sparkly green sleeveless thing and pulled it on as she rushed towards the door. She twisted the lock and threw open the door and there was her sister smiling a smile straight out of a Colgate commercial. "Looking good, Kate," was the greeting of choice. Nikki leaned forward and hugged Katie tight. "If these pants don't get you laid, I don't know what will."

Katie gave her sister a once over as they broke their embrace. It was typical Nikki. For Katie, a visit with her sister was like looking into a mirror and seeing how hot she could be, if only being hot was her job too. Together they were, and would always be, the walking, breathing embodiment of many a New England man's fantasy. They were twin redheads, firm but curved, lasses just as comfortable in the pub as they were when brought home to meet Mother. Katie knew she wasn't chopped liver, but it was only alongside her sister that she felt truly sexy, truly attractive. Hot by proxy.

Nikki wore her lengthy auburn curls up, piled atop her head in a carefully constructed coif; even the strand that fell across her face was absolutely calculated. Nikki loved to show off her neck. It was just long enough and the precision with which it curved into her shoulders was the work of a master sculptor. She wore tight black vinyl and left just enough to the imagination to assure her dance card would be full all night long. The shiny halter-top she wore was tied around the back of her neck and held her breasts firm, and as the cold Maine air rushed into the apartment from behind her, you could make out the barest outline of her nipples.

"Quit gawkin," Nikki advised as she made her way into the apartment and towards the fridge. She opened the heavy old refrigerator door and pulled out a bottle of Veryfine Fruit$_2$O. "You look just as good. We're gonna kill 'em tonight."

Katie turned and took a look into the full-length mirror she'd hung in the living room. She hadn't even taken time to check herself out. *Nikki was right*, Katie thought to herself. *I look just as good.* Out of habit, she went up on Pointe and did a pirouette. All that fighting with the jeans had paid off. Her ass looked irresistible. Her hair hung loose to her chin, and it didn't look all that awful considering she hadn't done a thing with it. The shirt wasn't bad either, except for where it clung too close and her bra became something of a feature attraction.

"How do you get yours to do that?" Katie queried.

"How do I get my what to do what?" Nikki responded, standing behind her, searching the mirror for Katie's source of dismay.

"Your boobs. How do you get them to stay so, so, you know, without a bra? Mine look awful without a bra. They sag."

" They do not. Take the bra off. I'll prove it to you."

"No. You've got the better boobs. I accept that."

"We got the same breasts, babe. We got size from Mom and firmness from Grandma. We've got virtual perfection in the breasts department."

"I don't think that's how it works."

"Shut up and take off the bra." Nikki raised an eyebrow with dissatisfaction.

Katie reached both of her hands behind her back and slid

them up under her shirt, unclasping the damned undergarment in one fluid movement. She pulled the strap off her left shoulder, then her right. Through the right side of her top, she pulled the bra, and then she dropped it to the ground.

From behind, Nikki cupped Katie's breasts and Katie's eyes shot open. "Hey! What are you doing?"

"Now, in my business, I cup about twenty pairs of these a week. At least twenty. And based on that experience, on my working knowledge of mammary glands, I can very safely tell you that these are not saggy tits. They've got at least another fifteen years of perkiness in 'em. Unless you have kids. Then you lose about ten years... but I've always thought you would be a good mom. Lot better than me I'd expect."

"Hey, sis, could you take your hands off my breasts? I know you get paid time and a half for it regularly, but this isn't exactly my idea of fun."

Nikki released her sister and came round front again. Nikki shook her head. "I don't know what you're talking about, Kate. I know girls at the club who would kill for a rack that stacked."

"A rack? Listen to yourself. You're talking more and more like your clientele every day. Your talent is going to waste in that place. Come up and dance here. Dance with me over in Dover."

"Listen to me? Ha! Listen to you! Do you really enjoy that shit? How many times can you take class with the same bunch of talentless yahoos you've been dancing with since Mom enrolled you back in kindergarten? How many times are you going to do that to yourself before you realize that you're the one who's talents are going to waste? You're wastin' your life away in Maine. And it's not even like you live in Portland. At least that would be a step in the right direction. Instead, you choose to perform to forty-five, fifty people tops at some little shack across the border in a town that's only slightly less hick-filled than this place."

"I happen to love South Berwick."

"And I happen to love Salisbury. I love being able to run on the beach every morning and I love the money I make at Tens. And I even love dancing naked, Katie. You know why? I'm proud of my body. You remember what Mom used to tell us: your body is your instrument, be proud of it, and play it loud. I'm playing it loud."

"And you're saying that I'm not proud of my body?"

"If you were proud of your body, you'd be dancing at the Wang in Boston, or the Schubert, or maybe even some place in New York. Your name would be in lights, or at least in a shiny new copy of *Playbill*, and I would be there every night with a dozen roses. Because I would do anything, anything, to see you take your instrument and wail away on it."

Katie plopped down onto the ratty old orange couch. "I don't want to go out anymore."

Nikki crouched down in front of her, hands on Katie's knees to comfort. "I didn't mean to hurt your feelings."

"I know," Katie said, head still hanging low.

Nikki lifted her sister's chin up. "Let's go out."

Katie stared into her sister's smiling Irish eyes, trying to make her decision, perhaps to find it within them. "Okay," was all she could muster.

❧

As SHE BUCKLED her safety belt and sunk into the passenger's seat of Nikki's newish green Beetle, she smiled. She needed to get out of her sleepy hamlet, if only for the night, and she was glad Nikki had convinced her to do so. This evening out demanded a locale where it would be impossible to hear herself think. Even prior to Nikki's accusation, Katie had a sense that deep thought should not be in the cards.

They jetted out of South Berwick, driving faster than was

allowed by law, and most definitely faster than was condoned by common sense. Katie wasn't eyeing the speedometer, but it seemed like something ridiculous. Maybe it just seemed crazy because, as quickly as a Schwinn 10-speed could carry you, she was sure a Volkswagen was a little bit faster.

THERE WAS little traffic and even littler chatter as they barreled down the interstate. At the Hampton tolls on the border of New Hampshire and Massachusetts, about twenty minutes down the highway, there was a frantic search for a dollar bill that had fallen somewhere in the front seat. But, that crisis resolved, they fell back into silence for the rest of the ride, all the way through the turn on to I-93, which brought them into Boston, where hopefully a night's worth of excitement awaited.

They parked at Malden Center station, a commuter rail and subway stop about fifteen minutes outside of the city. They took the orange line subway in. As much as she fit the part of the City Mouse, Nikki hated driving into Boston. Its built from the center roadmap and its Big Dig renovation project made her nauseous.

They took the orange line to North Station and got off in hopes of finding the green line connection right there as the signage had promised. They soon realized that even the subway in Boston, one of the country's first underground transit systems, was now a monument to inefficiency. Up the escalator and out the door they went, and there was no green line. It was a block away, the man in the little booth told them, and a block of walking in four-inch heels later, they had to pay up for another token to the obese black woman behind that counter, with her Coke-bottle glasses, bad teeth, and even worse acne. She hid in her little glass booth as Nikki fumed, using every four-letter word in her vocabulary to belittle the woman. Katie pulled her sister away, delivered the two dollars for their fare and guided Nikki through the turnstile.

On the platform waiting, Nikki was still pissed off. "I hate this city. I hate this city so fucking much, Kate. I mean it, if it weren't for Landsdowne Street, this place'd be a virtual landfill."

Katie smirked, "You do realize that most of this city really is a landfill don't you?"

"What are you talking about?"

Katie shook her head as the green line train squealed into the station. The sound of the decrepit old trolley pulling in and putting on its brakes was enough to make a girl's ears bleed. The speaker system in the club could probably boast the same thing, but that was more decibels than tonality. The green line arriving was like listening to a Yoko Ono record with the treble turned way up.

They spent fifteen minutes on the green line wedged between a toothpick of man devouring a bag of sour cream and onion potato chips and his slightly overweight friend, a man with the highest, most obnoxious falsetto Katie had ever heard. Then, finally, they were there. Up the stairs and out into Kenmore Square they raced, trying to get the memory and the scent of those two men off of them. All that was left between them and the blur of alcohol and gyrating she'd been anticipating all week was a seven-minute walk and a little flirting with the doorman.

The club was full, like a soon-to-be mother at nine months, about to burst at the seams with life and all the potential and energy that came with it. With a Screwdriver in one hand and a freshly lit Marlboro in the other, Katie had all but shaken the commute from her memory. She didn't smoke, except when she drank, and she didn't drink, except with her sister.

Katie stood at the edge of the dance floor, waiting for a song she could dig her heels into. Nikki was at her side with her first catch of the night. The guy was grinning like a wide-mouth bass, hook firmly implanted in cheek.

Nikki liked to torture them. If they could get through her five-minute diatribe on the indictment of organized religion in Lewis Carroll's, "The Walrus & the Carpenter," a speech she'd lifted from one of her favorite films, then she'd allow them a dance. If they could offer anything intelligent to the conversation —and she had strict guidelines when it came to intelligent contributions—she might give them a hand-job under the table in some darkened booth off in the corner, like she used to do for the boys at the roller rink, freshman year of high school. The more a guy stimulated her intellectually, the more likely she was to stimulate him in other ways, later on.

The energy of the crowd excited Katie. From Thursday to Sunday, hundreds of sweat-glistened dancing machines filled the club beyond capacity. This was what dancing was supposed to be: tribal, communal—every body, regardless of talent, shaking their moneymaker. Of course the technician in her did hope for a few more black men with their sense of adventure and their willingness to try any move once, and it made her wish for a few less white guys trying for a cheap score with their arms at their sides, tilting their head back and forth, doing their white guy dance. Out of the massive, sweaty throng, Katie spotted only one Caucasian face, and ass, that broke the mold.

He was thin and wiry, with a shag of blonde hair, uncut, though uncut in a precise, styled-to-be-messy way. A tight white turtleneck sweater clung to him, and he wore black leather pants form-fitting enough to accentuate his moves, but not so uncomfortably hip-hugging that he could immediately be pegged as a token gay guy, brought along to keep the demonic heterosexual men at bay. He danced like a gay man though, tapped into that feminine, creative side in a way that most straight men never could.

The girl that was with him, a petite brunette with a thick nose, was struggling to keep up. She'd assumed she'd be able to handle this one, like she could with all the others. She was winded though, and the perspiration was clumping her hair together and expelling the perfume from her pores. Judging by the look on her face, she'd obviously hoped to leave the sweating till later.

When Big Nose made eye contact with him, she smiled, but when she looked away her face contorted so that it looked like some sort of succubus had taken possession of her soul. Katie giggled at the girl as she counted the seconds till the song was over and then excused herself, fleeing towards the ladies' room to powder her nose, which, judging by the size of it, would keep her occupied for quite some time.

Blondie looked around but could not find a suitable partner, and so he started in Katie's direction. She gulped at her Screwdriver, nervousness overtaking her. The vodka and schnapps overpowered the OJ by a considerable margin. He might not even see her. There was a lot of club to navigate, and too many turns he could make to be sure, but as he waded through the sea of pulsating humanity, and as he passed over escape route after escape route, it became clearer and clearer that he was coming her way.

She was sweating like a pig and she hadn't even danced with him yet. She prayed that the ample supply of Secret Extra Dry and fuzzy peach perfume she'd applied earlier would mask the nervousness. She needed a reflective surface. She was convinced something was wrong with her hair, her lipstick, or something else, if not one or both of those things. If she took her eyes off of him though, they might not meet, *and God, think of the consequences then*, she thought to herself. Her vibrator had run out of batteries a week back, and without it she'd probably end the night with carpal tunnel syndrome after imagining what could have been with this prime cut of 98% fat-free beefcake. Katie took one last solid drag off her cigarette and extinguished it in the glass tray on the nearby table.

He grew closer, came more into focus. His shirt highlighted small but defined pecs, and abs that could neither be described as a six-pack, or a potbelly. He was toned but not muscled under-neath the T-shirt, which she'd misidentified as a sweater from afar. Katie wondered how much sweatier he would be if it was indeed a sweater, and how much she'd like to peel that sticky thing off of him and drink him all in. Oh, how she'd love to run her hands over that body, and slide them down inside those unyielding leather trousers.

Even a dance with Patrick Swayze straight out of *Dirty Dancing* would not sate her now, after that thought. She could feel her wrist throbbing already.

He made his way through the final herd of people and stopped, not merely brushing up against her, which is all she'd expected or truly hoped for, but stopping dead in his tracks to feast his eyes.

He asked, in a deep baritone that would have melted the panties of any woman in the club, if any of them were actually wearing panties, "Aren't you—?"

"Aren't I who?" She wondered aloud.

He smiled broadly and Katie noted a small chip on his left front tooth. His teeth were the color of a thrice-worn and not yet washed white shirt, just yellowing, but not yet disgusting enough for the before picture in a Rembrandt whitening toothpaste advertisement. His eyes were hazel, a peculiar shade that seemed to change from blue to green and back again with each blink.

"Of course, you wouldn't remember. You probably give a few dozen a night," he snickered.

She tilted her head to one side, a strobe pulsing at her, squinting her eyes for her. What the hell was he talking about? "A few dozen what?"

His cheeks reddened ever so slightly and he raised an eyebrow while he chuckled. In a whisper, so inaudible it might only have been his lips mouthing the words, he said, "Lap dances."

She bit her lip, yelling at herself within the confines of her mind, *He thinks I'm—Shit! And here I was, thinking this was my lucky day.*

"Oh," she said aloud, feeling the heat rush from her crotch to her forehead, as if someone had taken that warm apple pie and pushed it into her face like in an old Three Stooges short. "That must've been—" She turned to tap Nikki on the shoulder, to introduce her and give up the prize, so that at least one of them could get laid tonight. She turned to where her sister had been, and lo and behold: no Nikki.

"That must've been what?" he queried.

She looked all around her, into the abyss of bodies writhing in time to some teenybopper diva backed by a Swedish producer's *blurp* and *beep* rhythm section, but there was no Nikki to be found.

No Nikki. It was a unique opportunity. She wondered to herself as he waited for his answer, *I mean, when was the last time I got some? That guy a year and a half ago?* She recalled no more specific detail of him than the strange upward curvature of his penis and how little it pleased her, despite his many attempts to the contrary.

She smiled tentatively, hoping that her Barq's Root-beer addiction had not yellowed her teeth as completely as whatever had yellowed his had. Then, she said, "That must've been the only one I do remember from that night."

His mouth agape, he asked a bit too loudly, "You remember that?"

"I'd remember that, honey!" belted a woman from a table close by. Katie paid her no mind, thinking to herself, *I gave him a lap dance, bitch. He's all mine.*

"I do remember." She placed her hand on his leg, leaning in.

"You're just being nice."

"I am not. I mean, I am being nice, but that's because I don't want you to run off on me."

"I suppose it's not every day that you have a former customer spot you out in public."

She giggled, brushing a fallen hair away from her face, back behind her ear. "It is something of a rarity."

He looked at her, puzzled, squinting in the throbbing blues, greens, and reds of the club lights. Noticing something. "You cut your hair."

She tried not to let her eyes grow too enormous. The jig was up. *Don't look shocked Katie. It's been twenty-four hours at least, right? I could have gotten a haircut in a day.*

"You look great," he added. "Should I not have mentioned it? I like it a lot. It's hot."

She gritted her teeth to keep her jaw from lazing open-mouthed, and she swallowed a deep swig of oxygen, saliva, and fear. The acid, which had fought its way out of her stomach and up her esophagus, simmered down.

"Would you like to dance?" he asked.

She did, but she was petrified. Would she trip all over this guy? He was so good. "I don't know if I could keep up. I saw you. You're like a maniac out there."

"C'mon! You dance for a living. You're the pro. I'm an amateur. You shouldn't be intimidated by my moves."

"I don't know."

"Never thought an exotic dancer could be this shy," he said. "How long you been standing here?"

"A while." Hands on her hips, defending herself. *You talkin' to me?*

"C'mon, you're looking mighty fine tonight, and this crowd could use some more people who know what the fuck they're doing. I may be an amateur, but these people hardly even qualify to be called that. Let's dance!"

She looked at him. A trout swimming too close to the surface he was, begging to be caught. *I'm pretending to be Nikki. So, let's do what she would do.*

Without speaking, Katie grabbed his right hand, whirled him around, and sped towards the dance floor. His fingers, though thin and wiry like the rest of him, were each calloused at the tip. *A guitar player, perhaps?* If not for his otherwise boyish exterior, she might have imagined some other occupation: a construction worker, or a machinist. But no, he seemed like the artist type. A guitar player. Definitely.

As they fought their way through the masses, she imagined him and his fingers playing her like he played his guitar: one hand on the head and neck of her, fingering the right chords, massaging her, running his fingers through her locks; while the other hand strummed her below, first slowly, precisely, and then with ferocity. Her heart would provide the rhythm section in perfect 4/4 time, 120 beats per minute and speeding up, the first hand moving down her neck, further down the trunk of her, pulling from her higher notes each inch he descended, until she was screaming for him as both hands worked the same small area.

They found their place in the crowd just as the teen-queen and her Scandinavian-produced backbeat were coming to an end. The DJ was segueing into something harder, a techno instrumental. It was icy mechanical music, and now, with no warmth coming from the speakers, it was up to the crowd to stoke the fire themselves.

Katie loved techno because it was simple. Drum machine, synth bass, and an orchestra hit thrown in once a measure for the hell of it. There was very little song to the song. It made it harder to dance to, or at least harder to dance interestingly to. Like sex. When all that was left were the two people and their bodies and the rhythm they themselves created, very few people could have good sex. You needed candles and music and wine to create atmosphere. A truly great lover, or dancer, needed nothing more than the simplest beat to heat up a room.

Katie and her man circled each other at first, sizing up their prey, and then he tugged her into him. She straddled his left leg and they sank down and back up again. Her hand clutched his neck, and she threw her head and shoulders backward, grinding against his leg. His hand slid to the small of her back and he pulled her up and they stared at each other, panting a bit. His eyes had settled on green under these lights, and if she could dance the way his eyes made her feel at that moment, it would have been the greatest dance she'd ever danced. An X-rated dance, or at the very least an NC-17, but something more suited for Nikki's place of work than the performance space in dopey old Dover for sure.

Their eyes locked for an extended moment and then off of his leg she went, and spun around was she, her ass pressed against his crotch, her arm thrown up behind her, around his neck, drawing his face, his mouth, and his lips to her own neck. They moved like this for not long; she felt him growing hard against her. The dance was moving too fast. He was overheating too soon, and so she broke them apart and turned herself about to face him.

They fell into another groove and this time the game was to get as close as possible without touching. There wasn't much room to work with and the force of the people dancing around them made the game challenging, but they twisted and turned shoulders, hips, and arms, and every inch of themselves right down to their feet. They moved so fast that no camera could capture every intricacy. That was the heart of good dance. It couldn't be captured. Dance was a perishable art form. Music could be notated and paintings were paintings. Theatre had scripts and the director's promptbook, but dance was different. Neither he, nor she, would remember these moves the next day. They would remember the feeling. Dance was the truest of the art forms because everyone could move, and at the end of the dance you were never bogged down in details, like at a play trying to remember the line that made you laugh. You just came out of it with the feeling.

The song pulsed on, and it was near the end as the DJ faded smoothly into another beat, that Katie spotted her sister amidst the crowd. There Nikki was, descending from the bar area post haste, past the brunette and her mammoth beak. She was nursing a Sam Adams, standing amongst a gaggle of blonde co-eds who were sizing up a threesome of built black men in jean jackets. The co-eds were themselves being sized up by what must have been a trio of MIT computer geeks, though only one of them wore horn-rimmed glasses. There, in the middle of all that was Nikki, looking for something, or someone. Katie knew that she was probably the sought-after face in the crowd, if only just this once.

Katie grabbed her man's hand and went up on tiptoe, almost on Pointe, and whispered to him, "Let's get out of here."

He took her hand and whisked her through the crowd, arms like debris, flying this way and that. It wasn't until they were outside and he was unlocking the door of a white Jeep Cherokee that she remembered her purse was still in the club.

"Where are we going?" he asked as he held the passenger's side door open for her.

Fuck the purse! She thought to herself smiling. "Your place?"

He grinned and the chip on his tooth and the light yellow tint of his smile began to grow on her. He was rugged, she decided, battle-worn, not just a slob incapable of basic hygiene.

"Alright," he said as she stepped up into the car and took her seat. She fiddled with her seatbelt, which didn't want to come loose. He closed her door for her, ran round the front of the car and hopped into his own seat. Keys in the ignition, he put it into gear, pulled away from the curb, and they were off.

"How'd you get such a good parking spot?" She queried.

"My band was playin' down the street earlier tonight."

His band! I was right. "What do you play?"

"Oh, me? I don't play anything, really. I mean, I do play, but I'm just the guitar tech and the gear chauffer for this band." He motioned to the back seat. She hadn't noticed until he said something but the back seat was full of equipment: a full drum set, a few amps, and a ratty old guitar missing two strings. It looked like it had been salvaged from a junkyard.

"Pretty crappy-looking guitar," she commented.

"What, the flying V? Yeah, it's just for show. The thing doesn't even work plugged in. The lead singer's kind of a weirdo, one of those art-rock types. Absolutely insists on having the ax slung over his shoulder, but never fucking plays it."

"And you just left all this stuff out there unguarded?"

"For two songs. I love being part of a band, even if it isn't my own, but those guys are pretty damn pretentious and after the show I like to go on over and dance all their shit out of my system. Then I go home."

"Except tonight, you're not going home alone." She smirked.

"What makes you think I usually go home alone?"

She laughed. "Do you have a cell phone?"

He reached across her and into the glove box. "You're not going to phone China or something, are you?" He fumbled around inside the darkened compartment with no luck. "It's in there somewhere."

She pointed out the front window before resuming the hunt herself. "Keep your eyes on the road. I don't sleep with paraplegics."

He chuckled. "Hot girl like you isn't handicap-accessible?"

"Just don't get us into an accident, okay?" she said as she pulled the cell phone out from the darkness and clutter of car repair receipts and old audiocassettes.

She dialed Nikki's number quickly. Katie wanted this part over with fast.

"Hello?" came the voice after a quick three rings.

"It's me," said Katie.

"You ditched me, sis. He'd better be a catch."

Katie smiled at her blond stud, who was keeping his eyes finally, obediently, on the road. "He is."

"How you gonna get home?"

Katie grinned. "I don't know."

"Call me if you need anything."

"I will."

"And be careful, Kate. It's not exactly like riding a bike."

"How would you know?"

"Good point."

"You could have won the Tour de France three times over with all the riding you've done."

"That was cold, sis. We'll see how much pity I give you when you can hardly walk tomorrow."

"Love you."

"Love you, too."

Katie pressed END and tossed the phone back into the glove box.

"Who do you love?" the stud asked.

"Is that some sort of cheap pick-up line?" said Katie. "You don't need to pick me up, honey. In case you hadn't noticed, I'm already here."

"No. I was asking who was on the phone. Who do you love on the phone? Boyfriend? Husband?"

Katie ran her fingers through his hair. It was as soft as it was voluminous. She shook her head at him, "Nothing like that at all."

"Good, cause I don't get down with taken women. Nothing personal, it's just a thing of mine."

"It was my sister." She withdrew her hands, leaving his smooth locks behind. "I'm not the cheating kind either." And then there was silence.

He made a turn onto I-93 north, ascending the ramp onto the interstate. "What was your name again? I recall a lot about that night, but the name seems to have left me."

"Katie," she muttered, almost under her breath.

"Good thing I didn't guess then. Thought it was Vicki or Nikki or something."

Katie gulped, the subtle dangers of her subterfuge making

themselves known once again. She put her hand on his thigh and slid it up his leg towards his crotch. "No. It's Katie, and you best remember that when you're screaming it tonight."

"I usually stick to 'Oh God!' Its safer."

"You men, always afraid to take risks." She moved her hand the rest of the way up and began to rub him through the black leather, and she was sure there was no underwear now. She hadn't been positive before, but now she could feel the heat of him, and the spot where the head lay, and every ridge of his shaft. His pants hadn't seemed so thin until that moment.

"Jesus," he moaned. "It's going to be a long ride."

"How long?" she asked in the smokiest, dirtiest voice she could muster.

"Lowell."

"I can't wait that long. Pull over."

"What do you mean, 'pull over'? Where are we going to do it? The back seat is full of gear."

"That's what front seats are for. Pull over."

The blinker clicked on and he pulled over into the breakdown lane. As he did, she unzipped his pants and fought his penis out of them. Its girth was average, and the length, while nothing to write home about, would do. He put the car in park and turned off the lights.

"Now this is just an appetizer," she said, lowering her head down towards his lap, careful not to hit the steering wheel. She looked up at him for a second and said, "I trust you would have told me if I had anything to worry about here."

He nodded. "I would have."

She smiled and got to business, her tongue working at him like a snake charmer, circling the tip, calling forth that first trickle of moisture. His organ was under her spell and then she swallowed him into her mouth as far as she could go. The head tickled the back of her throat and she felt herself about to gag, but the moan he made kept her there a second longer. She pulled herself off of it and then lapped at his cock while she closed her fist around it, his hips rising and falling at her command.

It wasn't until they heard the knock at the window that they noticed the flashing white and blue lights. She snapped her head up to see what was going on and this time she did hit the steering wheel. She sat upright, rubbing the back of her head and then licking her lips to rid them of the evidence. Blondie rolled down the window and there was Officer Arlington, if she'd read right, crouching to match their wide-eyed stares.

"Having a little fun, kids?" the officer asked, as Blondie stared straight forward now, his cheeks pallid. She knew she'd gotten him hard, but she'd never imagined that she'd drawn enough blood down there to whiten his face so.

"Now, normally, I'd just let this slide," the officer advised them. "My wife and I done the same thing couple of times years ago. But this particular situation is a little more illegal than that."

"How's that, Officer?" Katie wondered aloud.

"Don't play dumb with me, Miss. Your boss is required by law to explain to you the rules. You don't look like the dumb type."

"What are you talking about?" she asked, still watching her newfound beau out of the corner of her eye, who truly looked like he'd seen an apparition of some kind.

"Partaking in sexual relations with the customers of your establishment is very illegal. It's what they call prostitution, Ms. Knockers."

Blondie came back to life, "Your stage name, Katie! It's Nikki Knockers. I think you should stop playing with the nice officer and cooperate."

"Waitaminute! My name's not Nikki Knockers. My name is Katie O'Donnell. Nikki Knockers is my twin sister."

The officer shook his head. "I'm getting really tired of your bullshitting, ma'am."

"No! I'm serious. This guy mistook me for my sister and I played along. I had to. I haven't had sex in a year and a half."

"You lied to me?" Blondie accused.

"Yes, and you pay women to shake their tits for you, so let's not question my moral fiber here."

"Could you both please step out of the car?" the officer requested, pulling at the driver's side door handle.

Katie opened her door, circled round the front end of the Jeep and put her hands on the hood while the officer patted her down. "Officer," she said, "how, may I ask, did you know that he was a customer?"

"Police officers have libidos too, Ms. Knockers."

"Then you should know that the customers aren't allowed to touch the entertainment, especially not like this."

"Very funny. This guy is in there more often than I am, but I'm surprised you don't remember me. I've always been a reasonably good tipper. I'm a big admirer of your work." He started to pat Blondie down. "The new haircut is quite striking."

She sighed as he cuffed her, "Aw, thank you, Officer."

THE PROCESS of being processed wasn't nearly as painful as she'd imagined, though the smell of the drunken vagabonds sitting inside the holding cell was quite unbearable in and of itself. A pudgy prostitute with hair the color of dried December grass asked Katie if she worked Washington Street too, because she looked familiar.

It was forty-five minutes between her phone call and the time Nikki arrived to pick her up, forty-five minutes of crying and catfights straight out of some pro-wrestling show. Nikki explained the whole situation and signed autographs for the officers, and after ten minutes on the green line and ten on the orange, they were in the car, keys in the ignition, just sitting there. Nikki was shaking her head, perhaps hoping that the words would just fall out. "Kate, why did you do it?"

Katie gazed out ahead, eyes locked on the taillights of a Chevy Chevette in front of them backing out of its spot. *Who the hell still owns a Chevette?* she wondered, trying to distract herself as Nikki repeated her question. She had no answer.

"Kate, there were probably a good hundred guys in that club tonight that would have gone for you. That guy might have even been into you if you had told him the truth."

"Wouldn't have changed the fact of me getting caught giving him a blowjob on the side of 93."

"It might have, Kate. I mean, that's not a Katie thing to do. That's a Nikki thing. I don't think you would have done it if you haven't been so wrapped up in playing a part."

"So what if I pretended to be you, Nik? Guys don't like girls like me. They don't like awkward girls. I don't know how to be sexy. I don't know how to turn a guy on. At most, guys want to be friends with me. They certainly don't want to sleep with me."

"It's just like the dancing, Kate. You dance the way Mom danced, in the places she danced. You siphon her energy, and summon her spirit, because you have no confidence in your own ability. You have so much to offer, Kate, but you keep it all buried inside, and then you hide yourself away in the woods in Maine."

Katie bit down on her lower lip, trying to hold back the tears, to sandbag the floodgates and keep them from running over.

"I go to performances in Portsmouth and Portland, and even sometimes here in Boston and I see lots of dancers. But never once have I seen one with the same passion for it as you. Sure, they can pirouette. They've had their bodies programmed since they could stand up and fit into a tutu. And it's amazing to watch them, sort of like it's amazing to watch a gymnast, to ask yourself, 'How did they do that?' But when you dance, when you move Kate, it's magic. You cast a spell. And it pisses me off that I am the only one that gets to see that."

Katie sat in her seat, her head ducked and her lip sore, her best work to keep the tears back all for naught. She sobbed hard, gasping and grabbing at breaths, almost suffocating herself on her tears. *Nikki's harsh, but she's right.* Katie searched her purse for a Kleenex as Nikki navigated the streets of Malden, making their way back out to the highway.

They'd reached the rotary that could take them either way on I-93. The first right was marked '93N, Lawrence' and Nikki was navigating towards it when Katie yelled, "No! Don't go that way!"

"What? What are you talking about?" Nikki swerved off of her predetermined path and back onto the rotary proper, much to the dismay of the car behind them, who answered their sudden change of direction with a hail of honking and high beams.

Katie remained silent as they lapped the rotary again. Nikki fumed, "Listen, sis, you might like getting pulled over—I'm sure it's a breeze as a passenger—but I don't feel like having to explain to one of the cops I just spent buttering up with fifteen minutes of autographs and cleavage why I was doing laps around the rotary. Why the hell did you want me to stop?"

"Because we're going south."

"I am not driving into Boston."

"No you're not. We're driving through Boston. We're driving to Providence."

"Excuse me?" Nikki questioned as they passed the 93N exit for a third time.

"I have a couple of friends I graduated with that are trying to get a company started down there. They asked me to join at graduation, but I went off to be at Mom's side. Then, when Mom died, I was so drained I just couldn't bring myself to go. You've inspired me, Nik. You've kicked me in the ass and woken me up. We're going to Providence."

"I'll drop you off somewhere but I am not going to stay."

"Oh, yes, you are. I need you Nikki. To keep me motivated. Besides there are ten times more clubs in Providence. Do you really think you're making what you deserve out there at the beach? You're Nikki Knockers, for Christ's sake, and you're working at some dive in the middle of nowhere. If I'm going big-time, so are you."

They passed 93N for the fourth time and then they rounded about again and there was 93S. Katie looked at her sister and Nikki looked back. They smiled and grabbed hold of each other's hand. Nikki turned the wheel and they were off, headed south, to Providence.

THOSE LITTLE BASTARDS

I was going to divorce him, but I didn't. I was going to sleep with this guy I work with, that always takes me out to lunch, always listens to my problems, always treats me the way I want to be treated. I was going to, but I didn't. You know, I was going to do a lot of things with myself but I just never did. I stuck by the asshole. I had two very good reasons.

The first reason we named Amber. The second we called Samuel. Those little bastards were my reasons. I loved them so damn much, and I didn't want anything to happen to them. They didn't need to see what I seen growing up. They didn't need to see their parents split up and bitter. I saw that. My kids didn't need to.

⚜

I MET him back in high school. I went to Chelmsford High and he went to the Tech over in Westford. I should've gone to the Tech. I wasn't cut out for regular high school. I woulda done good at a trade. My mom went to the Tech. Ain't no shame in it. But that's not the way my father saw it. He wanted more for me. He wanted me to get a good education and go off to college like him. He wanted me to go to his fancy liberal arts school up in Haver-hill there. He didn't want me having a diploma from some Tech school, goin' on to work in some grocery store like Mom.

My Dad didn't get me. I was just like Mom. I wasn't smart. I sure as hell wasn't gonna be cut out for college. Hell, I was so sure that I had gotten a bad score on my SATs that I didn't even bother to open the envelope when it came. I threw it in the back of my Bronco and drove off to my friend Linda's.

I stopped over at Harrington's first to grab a six-pack of Bud Ice. I wasn't of age yet, but I gave one of the clerks there a handjob once and he hadn't forgotten how good it was. I didn't go into the store. They wouldn't have let me in. Respectable place, that Harrington's. I didn't go into the store, but I didn't have to. I told him to meet me outside.

John came out of that store, strutted up to my truck, tossed the beer onto the floor on the passenger's side and got in. We knew someone in the store was watching him, so I decided to take him home rather than have him get back out and look suspi-cious. They took selling to minors very seriously. Still do, I hear.

I dropped John off at his house on North Road. John's family was more white trash than my mom's. There wasn't never a point I drove by there where they didn't have at least three cars up on blocks. They had done an addition to their house about ten years back and the damn thing still wasn't finished. Back in middle school, when I used to hang out with John's younger brother a lot, I saw the inside of the place and it was a Goddamn wreck. From the outside, it didn't look bad. From the inside, it looked like they hadn't even started yet. It was all plywood and two-by-fours, and half-installed insulation. Me and John's younger brother Frank, we got drunk on rum cake in the unfinished addition once while John and his pregnant girlfriend nursed Coronas and laughed at us.

With the beer on my floor and the new Nirvana record blaring through my car stereo, I sang along to "Rape Me" at the top of my lungs. It seemed just the sort of thing my father wouldn't want me to do.

At the party, you had the usual mix of regulars and oddball popular kids who hadn't been invited to that weekend's cooler get-togethers. Then there was that core group of us, the ones that most teachers regarded as the bad seeds, the stoner morons. The popular kids hung out with a couple of us, the more attractive, more normal-looking ones, because we could get them pot. Hey, it was high school. What-the-fuck-ever, you know? I sold pot to guys who went into the state senate, girls who are now vice presidents in Internet start-ups. I even sold pot to Garry Kent, the porn star. He went to CHS, too. He was one of our crew. Did a killer De Niro impression. Had a Joe Pesci that wasn't bad either. Always said he wanted to be an actor, but never tried out for any plays. I thought that was strange.

This scene, this is where I met my future husband. He was a cute metalhead by the name of Brian. I thought it was cool that he was still into that music when it was no longer cool to be into that music. He had long blond hair and he didn't go anywhere without his leather jacket, across the back of which was the Motörhead logo. He peered out at me from behind his glasses and he nodded, raising his can of Coors up in the air, a headbanger's hello.

I dumped my six-pack in the kitchen, said a few hellos, and went back into the living room. He was still sitting by himself in the corner nursing that Coors when I went over and sat next to him.

"Hey," I said. "You mind some company?"

He shook his head no and motioned for me to sit down.

I sat cross-legged on the floor in front of him and pulled out my battered pack of Marlboro reds. I offered him one first and he reached and pulled one out of the pack. I slid my own out, the last one, and crumpled the pack. Then, I watched the butt hang on his lip while he dug through his inside pocket for a light.

He lit us both up and we sat there smoking and taking turns sipping from his Coors. When the alcohol was gone and the butts had burned down to their filters, he stood up and reached his hand down to pull me up with him. I took his hand, pulled myself up, and followed him up the stairs.

🌀

AFTERWARDS, I felt stupid for not using a condom, but he was so damn good I just decided not to worry about it. He was passed out, facing away from me, and his thin body looked strange out of the leather. I hadn't noticed when we were going at it but he looked weaker without his gear on, more... I don't know... more something. He didn't look as tough. That was basically it.

I didn't see him again for a few weeks. We didn't go to the same school, after all, and with midterms coming up I was really fucking busy. I mean, I didn't give two shits about school or nothing, but I didn't want to repeat the eleventh grade, y'know. I hated one of my teachers. The guy I had for English was a real prick. He was a complete Shakespeare nut and he had us reading all this old stuff that I just didn't get. I didn't want to deal with him for another year, so I took my midterms seriously for the first time in my life. I had to get promoted to the next grade. No question about it.

It was at the end of those couple of weeks that I started to get nervous. I had never been regular, y'know, in terms of my period, but it was starting to get ridiculous. The thought did cross my mind once or twice that I might be, y'know, but I never thought too long about it. I couldn't handle that shit at that moment.

The weekend after midterms, it still hadn't come. It had been six weeks since my last period and I was worried. After school that next Monday, I walked over to Drum Hill and bought a home pregnancy test at the drug store over there. I took it in the bathroom of the McDonalds on the other side of the road, after woofing down a cheeseburger and throwing it right back up. I waited and waited and I cried the whole damn time, hoping nobody would come in and hear me. When the stupid thing finally delivered the news, it wasn't what I'd expected.

I wasn't pregnant.

I got my period three or four hours later. I had never been happier for cramps and blood-stained panties in my life.

❦

BRIAN and I started seeing each other more often that summer. We drank a lot of beer, smoked a lot of pot, and had ourselves more sex than was probably necessary. His Dad was out of the picture and his Mom never bothered us, never asked what we did up in his room for hours on end. She loved her son and she was constantly afraid of losing him. He threatened to take off a lot and so she never asked questions. As far as I can tell the big mess started on September 3, 1994, couple days before the start of senior year. The sex was rough that day, the way I liked it, and well, the fucking condom broke. We panicked and we fought and he told me to leave. I walked the five miles from his house in Westford to mine in Chelmsford, couple streets over from the Town Hall.

We never really broke up, but then again we were never going out, not like most high school kids go out. We hung out with each other. We kissed. We screwed. It was a relationship, but we never had a label for it. We were through though, after that; at least that's the way I saw it at the time.

❦

THE PERIOD DIDN'T COME that time. I waited a little longer to freak out. It was about Halloween when I walked into that same drugstore, bought that same test, and walked over to that

McDonalds again to see what was going on. I didn't have the cheeseburger that time, but I still threw up. I had been nauseous a lot in the couple weeks before, mainly in the mornings.

Sitting in the stall of that McDonalds bathroom, I prayed for good news. I prayed for another bit of unexpected luck.

I didn't get it. I didn't get no luck that time. I was pregnant.

⚜

AT THE HALLOWEEN party Linda threw that weekend, everybody seemed to notice I wasn't drinking. They all asked what was up and I told them I just didn't feel like it. Brian was there, over in his corner, sipping beer with some redheaded bitch, smoking her cigarettes. She was his fifth girl since our breakup. The fucking prick, he glanced over at me once or twice. The second time, he gave me his metalhead hello. I didn't give him anything back.

I sat in the old brown recliner in the corner of the darkened living room for most of the night, trying to steer clear of the haze of cigarette smoke, only getting up to go to the bathroom and grab another can of Coke. Brian had disappeared up the stairs with his little redheaded bimbo about fifteen minutes after he gave me his hello. He'd been gone for two hours. The party was dying down. I was considering going home.

With my bag slung over my shoulder, I headed for the door and it was only at the last minute that he caught me. Brian grabbed me by the arm and I stopped. Looking at him and his face trying to figure me out, I wanted to slap him. I wanted to slap him till he was on the floor begging me to stop and then I wanted to kick the motherfucker in the balls, keep him from ever knocking anyone up again.

I wanted to, but I didn't.

"People tell me you ain't drinking," he said to me.

"I've got my reasons."

"And what are they?"

"Wouldn't you like to know?"

"I would."

"Why don't you go back upstairs to your new slut?"

He stared into my eyes and I stared right back. He squinted.

"You're pregnant," he deduced.

I looked away.

"You are, aren't you?" he asked.

I turned back to him and nodded.

He put his arms around me and pulled me close. It felt too damn good for me to consider pushing him away.

ॐ

IT WAS PROBABLY the strangest year of my life, that year. I'd never been given as much attention at school. Y'see, if I went to the Tech, or to like, Lowell High, it wouldn't have made any difference y'know? I wouldn't have been the only one. At CHS though, I was. I was the only pregnant girl there, and I got plenty of attention for it, good and bad.

It started with the staring. The girls stared because they thought I was a slut, because I exposed that there really were people at that school having fun, having sex, whatever. They hated me because, I mean, how could I do it? How could I tarnish their school's reputation? Girls got pregnant in the slums of Lowell or in the hills of Westford, but not in Chelmsford, not here.

The boys stared because they wondered if they could be the next to get the easiest lay at CHS into bed. I mean, nobody expected me to keep it. They all thought I was going to abort. They figured once the little shit was gone from my belly they could get their groove on with me. They'd use a condom, of course. Some of them would have used two, just to be safe. That's what they told their buddies. At least that's what I heard.

I didn't abort. With Brian back at my side, I decided to keep it. We weren't married and we had no plans to get married. In fact, our getting back together consisted of make-up sex and an understanding that we wouldn't sleep with other people, at least until the baby was born, more of commitment on his part than mine. I wasn't about to sleep with anything. I thought it would hurt the baby. Just one time with Brian was enough to keep me up all night sweating bullets until I got into the doctor's office the next day and she told me everything was alright. It was a big deal for him. Brian, like most men, loved sex. He couldn't get enough, and as nice a guy as he was, he'd never been able to stay faithful to any one girl in his entire life.

He did break his promise. It was only one time, but it was enough. She was a brunette and I found her giving him a blowjob in the front seat of my Bronco. He fucked around in my Goddamn truck! I told him I didn't want him around anymore and he left me alone until I called him up three days later and begged him to come back. I was unstable. I was in high school. I didn't know I could do any better.

THE NINE MONTHS were pure hell. Everything I did was major news for the Chelmsford rumor mill. There's one time, in particular, that I remember. Some kid accidentally elbowed me in the stomach on one of the crowded staircases at school and I had to be sent to the hospital as a precaution. It was April 5, a Wednesday. On the stretcher, I looked up and saw the sun peeking through the clouds and melting off a very late frost. I felt stupid. I knew nothing was wrong. Even as a first-time mother, I knew my baby was okay.

The kid who hit me didn't do it on purpose, but some of the people who were there thought that he had and so he was suspended. When I came back to school the next Monday, after two days off to recover from my 'ordeal,' nobody got near me. They didn't want to touch me, even brush against me.

It was nice to have a path cleared for me everywhere I went, nice for a few days at least. After those first few days, I knew what was going on. They weren't clearing a path for me. They were running away. I was like a circus freak to them, the tiger that was interesting in its cage but frightening when let loose. They'd been so intrigued when me being pregnant was just an idea, a conversation starter. Now that my belly was bulging, they wanted to be as far away as possible.

❦

LUCKILY, that last three months went by fast with all the doctor's appointments and finals and getting ready for graduation. I'd managed to earn a 2.3 GPA overall, much better than I'd expected of myself at the beginning of the year, but a far cry from the three-point-whatever my father had been hoping for.

My mom threw me a last minute baby shower in the back room of the diner she'd started working at after the grocery store was sold to a bigger company and she was laid off. My father was pissed. He had wanted me to abort it right away. In fact, the only thing he enjoyed about the situation was that he had a new drinking buddy in Brian, even if he was only eighteen and drinking with him was a criminal offense.

Everything started to fall into place. Graduation was scheduled for Saturday June 3. My due date was the fourth. If all went well, I would be able to do both. Somewhere... somewhere in that last year, I had begun to care about school. It seemed to me nobody but my father ever thought I would amount to anything school-wise. That never bothered me. But when people started doubting me because of my pregnancy, because of my baby, that got under my skin. When those girls started looking at me like I was a waste, that pissed me off. That's when I wanted to prove them wrong. I was going to graduate and have my baby too. I was going to show them.

Well, as fate would have it, storm clouds were brewing on the evening of June 3 and graduation was postponed. I sat in my room that night, trying to keep myself occupied with a book of baby names and not having much success. Every name reminded me of a kid at school who I hated. I kept looking up at the murky sky, cursing it. Maybe the baby would come late. It had already been a miracle, the doctors told me, that baby hadn't come early. Maybe it wouldn't come until after the rescheduled graduation ceremony the next day. I put my baby name book on the nightstand, crossed my room, flicked off the light switch, and then crawled under my covers, hoping.

At three A.M., I was up again. My baby wasn't going to wait anymore.

THE REST of that warm June Sunday was sweat and screams and blood, a terrified soon-to-be grandfather who'd forgotten what it all looked like since his one and only experience eighteen years before; a beaming soon-to-be grandmother, happy that her daughter had taken her life into her own hands; and a soon-to-be father disgusted with himself for causing me so much pain.

When they cleared them all out of there and told me they were going to cut her out of me, I was scared. The blonde nurse who didn't look much older than me, she smiled and wiped my forehead with a cloth. The doctor talked to me in a voice he might've used to explain something to his five-year-old child. At the time, I thought it was because of my age; but when I had my second child a couple years later, they talked to me the same way. Now I'm convinced that's just the way they talk to women. I betcha they don't talk babytalk to another guy when they're tugging on their balls giving them a hernia exam.

The rest is a blur, even the minutes before they administered the anesthesia. I don't remember if they knocked me out or if they just made part of me numb. It seems to me that I was asleep, but I might have been awake. I don't know. Alls I know is that it was few hours of knowing my baby wasn't there anymore before they let me hold her, before they let me know it was alright. They told me later that I had held her for a second right after delivery, but I don't remember that.

What I do remember was the sight of her, of my little Amber, her face all red and wrinkled. She can still make that face when I send her to bed without TV because she's done something bad. The doctor told me she was a bit better off in the looks department for having been born the way she was, but none of that really mattered to me. She wasn't a very pretty baby, but she was beautiful just the same. I kept muttering to myself, "I made you... I made you."

And if that wasn't enough, if that wasn't enough to tug on my heart until it throbbed and pulsed and begged to be left alone, the next memory I have is almost as good. The nurse took Amber from me and placed her into Brian's arms, and it was that was the image I had in my head when he started coming home drunk and blaming his bad days on me, screaming it was all my fault. "I can't work on my music cause I gotta go out and support you." Or, "I slept with her because you don't get me off no more." When Brian held our little Amber in his arms, that was all the reassurance I ever needed. She cuddled up against his chest and he looked down at her through his thick locks, his thick glasses, and tears slid across his tough skin.

⁂

WE BROUGHT her home to my father's house a few days later and that was the same day my diploma arrived. Sitting, feeding my baby from her bottle—I refused to breastfeed my first out of stupid teenage vanity—I was shocked to see my boyfriend down on his knee, pulling a little felt-covered box from the inside pocket of his leather jacket. I didn't think the word 'commitment' was even in Brian's vocabulary. When he asked me that day, I wondered whether my father had put him up to it, but maybe it was the baby in my arms, or the thought of some real security, or maybe it was some craziness left over from being pregnant. I don't know what it was, but I said yes.

There was a small ceremony and reception that August. My Dad was more than happy to pay for it all. It was our families and Brian's friends from the Tech, and the few friends I had left from CHS, and it was an alright party except for all the running back into the house my mother had to do to feed and change the baby. "Better me than you," my mother explained a few times. "It's your wedding day."

Sammy came a year and a half later in January of 97, and it was during that pregnancy that it all started to hit the fan. Brian's cheating kept getting worse. He used to keep it to one girl at a time—two, if you counted me—but now he was... I just never understood why he couldn't keep his dick in his pants. The therapist told us that Brian had a sex addiction problem, that he had no desire to hurt me or the kids but he couldn't control his urges. Good old Dr. Robertson also told us Brian's dad probably abused him. Then Brian admitted his father started showing him Marilyn Chambers movies when he was eight and that's why, a couple of years later, his dad got kicked out. There were lots of nods between the two of them then, knowing glances. But me, I think sex addiction was invented by men to explain away screwing around. I let the therapist convince me, though. I let him convince me and I stuck. I had one very good reason at home, and another in my belly.

The New Year's Eve right before Sammy was born—and that was the day right before he was born, actually—Brian made a resolution to stop his screwing around. I didn't believe him, but I looked over at our sleeping child, then at my bulging stomach, and I let him convince me.

Two weeks later, when the cop came to our apartment and told me there had been a car accident and that my husband was dead, I didn't believe him. But when I looked into his eyes and he looked down to avoid my gaze, I knew. He wasn't lying.

I WAS GOING to divorce him. I had the papers to file for separation in my purse that night as I was walking up the steps of our building, had my fingers wrapped around them when the cop stopped me. I was sick of his excuses, of his breaking promises. I was finally sick of it all and willing to go it alone. I had two good reasons not to divorce him, but I was going to do it anyway. And then he had to go off and get himself killed.

I miss you, you unfaithful fuck. You couldn't keep your cock locked up where it belonged, but the way you held our kids—I won't ever forget that.

I won't ever forget that.

THE PERFECT PITCH

Her breasts were heavy and her vagina not especially tight. I picked the young ones for a reason, because they were easier to mold, because you could teach them to fuck the way you wanted to fuck. But this girl, this girl was already learned in the sack. A little too learned for my tastes. It wasn't what I was looking for.

Now, don't get me wrong. I'm not a pedophile or anything. I'm not looking for the really young ones. Eighteen is my cutoff. In fact, I don't even like going that young most of the time. You fuck them at eighteen and soon they're telling all their girlfriends about it and one of those girlfriends happens to be particularly close to her mother and she confides it all in her and then that mother, after debating with herself for a day or two, calls up your girl's mother and then it's just a big fucking mess.

Not that I'm speaking from experience.

This girl was a little different. She was part of the latest wave of teenaged music sensations, stopped over in Boston for a break in her summer tour. The world had hit that pathetic point in the cycle of pop culture, the point where the kids no longer care about music with substance and only bother devoting their attention to the latest, hottest-looking band. I was no big fan of grunge when it happened, but at least some of those bands could write songs. There was some music amidst all the bullshit. The same couldn't be said for the time when I was screwing this particularly loose girl.

She was a platinum blonde, though her coif must have been darker at one point based on the color of her pubic hair. Her patch was trimmed into a small arrow that pointed towards her genitals, instructions for the groupies who didn't know what to do with themselves after feasting their eyes on her nakedness. I wondered how long it would be until my daughter asked me if she could dye her hair that color, about how I would convince her not to do it without coming right out and telling her that dyeing your hair that color communicated only one thing: the wrong thing.

It was around that time that things began to become more difficult. My daughter's thirteenth birthday was coming up. Puberty was in full swing when she was at my house and I was dreading the day when I would have to go to the store and buy her pads because her mother had forgotten to. Guilt was a daily part of my routine. If I was fucking these girls now, whose fathers thought they were dropping them off for a piano lesson, what was to stop some perverted tennis instructor from sleeping with my little girl when she came of age? Or even before she came of age? Not all men take the time to set standards like I do.

All of this was racing through my head, at least to some extent, as I did that little blonde starlet from behind while she kneeled on my piano bench. She braced herself with her hands on the keyboard and every once in a while, when I got her just right, her fingers would leap up from the keys, fall down again, and strike a perfect C chord. It was faintly amusing that she moaned in harmony with the chords she struck.

It wasn't until she came that I really enjoyed myself, for as loose as she was during the majority of it, she clenched tighter than most at the end. I pulled out and I counted myself lucky as I let myself drip onto her back. I had almost come inside of her and that is where accidents begin. That's where my daughter had begun back in college, when controlling myself was the least of my worries.

The starlet took a quick shower in the downstairs bathroom, then came back in tight blue jeans and a vintage Madonna t-shirt to begin her lesson. The other teenage divas were all learning to play guitar, to expand their horizons and add a little something musical to their shows. She'd decided to be different and take up piano. It would be 'slamming,' she told me, if she could play piano on the live version of her latest record. The crowd would go nuts. I asked her why she'd chosen to take lessons here in Boston when she could've done so in L.A. or New York. She told me something about her ancestors coming from the Cape and how her great-great grandfather had moved his part of the family down to Jersey and how she liked coming up to Massachusetts because she felt a deep connection with her past up here. She went on for about fifteen minutes in that all-too excited voice of hers, and I was sorry that I asked.

On the plus side: my little starlet learned fast when we sat at the piano, and she took a real interest in everything I showed her. This I respected. It wasn't merely about how to look convincing on stage. She really wanted to learn.

That first lesson went quickly, ending when her handlers came knocking at the door, telling her she had a signing to go to. She said that she loved the way I taught and she would be back for another lesson in a week. I smiled and told her I would look forward to it.

⚜

EMILY, my daughter, came into my house in a tizzy that afternoon, complaining about how her mother wouldn't take her to some record signing in town before dropping her off with me. I asked her what signing she'd wanted to go to, and when she mentioned the name of my little starlet I steadied my jaw, told her I was sorry, and promised I'd take her out to do something cool that weekend.

She begged me, "Can't we go now, though? The signing's not over yet and if we hurry—"

"Why do you like her so much, Emily? What is it about these bands today that gets you excited?"

"She's really talented, Dad. And she's a good role model. She always talks about how she believes in God and how she'd never let a guy treat her the wrong way. She's even a virgin, Daddy. And that's saying something, especially in today's world."

Trying not to chuckle, I asked, "She's a virgin?"

Emily nodded.

"Em, I'm glad that you're considering the moral fiber of the people you look up to, but musically, I can't help but be a little appalled that this is the kind of stuff you like to listen to. I thought I'd taught you better."

"Mozart and Beethoven and Lennon and McCartney are okay, Daddy, but they're all dead."

"Paul McCartney's not dead."

"Jenna's Dad says he's dead. He says the guy who took Paul's place is named Billy Shears or something. It even says Paul's dead if you play their records backwards."

"I don't think you should speak with Jenna's father about music anymore."

"Whatever. I guess I'm trying to tell you that, like, I love the music you've had me listen to so far in my life, but that's not what's happening now. I like this girl, and all the others. Their music is fun. It makes me want to dance."

"Does it make you want to sing?"

"I don't want to sing, Dad. Only the geeky girls sing, the ones in chorus and music theatre, the dorky girls."

"You used to be friends with those girls."

"Yeah. In middle school."

"That was last year."

"You're right, Daddy. That was *so* last year." She paused. "So, can we go?"

I shook my head no, went back into my piano room, and closed the doors.

❦

AFTER AN HOUR of pounding out tracks from *The White Album* and *Abbey Road*, my disgust with my daughter's state of mind was out of my system. Out in the living room, she laid on the couch, talking on the phone with one of her friends and painting her toenails an absurd shade of pink.

I stood at the edge of that sofa, waiting for her to notice me; finally she did, and she smiled up at me as she said her goodbyes. Emily placed the phone back in its cradle, stood up, and hugged me. "I'm sorry, Daddy," she said.

"You don't have anything to be sorry about, Em."

"I know you think I'm wasting my gifts."

"You have a beautiful voice, Emily."

"And someday I'll use it, Daddy. Maybe someday I'll even become a big pop star like—"

She continued, but the moment she said pop star, then mentioned my starlet's name, the only words I heard were my own unspoken ones, the words, 'I hope not.'

I took Emily out to the California Pizza Kitchen on Stuart Street. Then we stopped in for a movie at the new Loews Cinema on Tremont. I don't remember what we saw, but I do remember that I fought for a movie that wasn't devoid of intelligence and I lost. My daughter was determined to be one with the mindless masses of her generation and I guessed there was nothing I could do to stop her. The only thing I could do was try to be less abrasive at the sound of her requests, so that she wouldn't run home to her mother screaming she didn't want to see me anymore.

❦

THE REST of our weekend together was a relatively normal one consisting of her having some friends over, going out to another movie with them, then finally humoring me by sitting down for a voice lesson on Sunday afternoon before her mother came to pick her up.

As we worked through pieces both contemporary and classical, I had to fight back tears. Emily had perfect pitch and her voice was more beautiful than anything I had ever aspired to. My little girl had more God-given talent in her than she knew what to do with, and really, she didn't know what to do with it at all.

We were finishing up when her mother rang the buzzer. Emily obliged me and finished the song before grabbing her things and leaving me with a kiss on the cheek. I turned back to the piano, casting pages of notation aside until I found the piece I'd been working on writing. I had four measures and none of them were very good, but I always came back to it anyway. It distracted me.

❦

THE REST of the week rolled by at the pace of a quadriplegic tortoise, the monotony of my daily lessons broken up only by some killer head from Nancy Monroe, an old student back from college for the summer. She'd become the star of the music theatre program up in Haverhill, at my alma mater, Kimball College, and as she knelt in front of me, licking the remnants of me from her lips, still holding on tight, I could see how.

I had a promising session with John Crane that Thursday, as well. John was possessed of these amazingly thin fingers that glided across the keys as if a ballerina on pointe. His lessons were always superb. I didn't have to give John much instruction and that was good. My thoughts were on my little starlet and not much else.

I watched out the window that Friday as her limo crept up Beacon Hill towards my brownstone. As frustrating as she had been at first, I found myself longing for her again after a week apart.

She came in as she had the week before, dressed in a long trench coat with a hood pulled over her head to hide her face. From the darkness of the hood, I saw her flash a smile. Then she threw off that coat and leapt up into my arms.

I held her up by her ass as she wrapped her legs around my waist and buried her face against my neck, biting at it until she had worked her way up to my ear. I carried her into the kitchen, pulled her blue jeans off and fucked her on top of the breakfast bar.

৩✦৩

ONCE AGAIN, her lesson went well. She learned fast and I imagined she wouldn't need much more from me. It was a sad thought at the time. As much as I had initially disliked the level of her experience, I had, after that second time, grown accustomed to screwing her. It wasn't all that bad, her carnal knowledge. I would miss it when she was gone.

When we were through working at her song, the one she wanted to perform, she stood up from the bench and stuffed her hands into her front pockets. She said something about how awesome it was to be learning so fast but my attention was elsewhere. Her pants hung loose around her hips and with her hands in her pockets pushing them even further down, I could see the tip of that thin strip of hair, that arrow of hers. I went behind her and slid my hand into the front of her jeans and I worked her that way as she threw her arms behind her and held my face to her own. I let my other hand work her breasts and I pinched at her nipples hard. She seemed to like that.

The starlet moaned with delight as I finished her off and then, despite the knocking at the front door—sure to have been her handlers coming back for her—she dropped to her knees and pulled my shaft from my pants. Just as she was beginning, I heard the front door unlock and open. I pulled my girl to her feet and zipped up my pants. What the hell were they doing?

I ran out of the piano room and my starlet followed behind, but when we got to the foyer her handlers were not there. No, the knocking and the abrupt entrance had been the work of someone else. There stood, with her jaw wide open, my Emily.

"Ohmigod." Emily stuttered. "Daddy, that's, that's—" She pointed at my girl and my girl smiled back. "What's she doing here?"

"She's come to take a lesson."

My starlet told Emily, "I stopped by once when I was on break from the tour and your Dad was such a good teacher that I decided to come back."

"You flew all the way from Dallas to Boston to take a piano lesson with my dad?" Emily wondered.

The starlet nodded her head yes. As she did, the knocking of her handlers finally came. "I've got to go," she told us. "Thank you," she told me.

Emily, awestruck, managed a few words. "Can I get an autograph?"

"I'll be back next Friday. I'll give you an autograph then. How's that?"

"That'd be awesome." Emily smiled.

"And maybe we'll talk a bit, afterwards."

Emily fanned herself with her hand, trying not to cry. "Ohmigod!" She shrieked and ran up to my girl and gave her a hug, and then, releasing her, stepped back towards me and watched the starlet go.

As the door closed, my daughter hugged me tighter than she had since she was a very little girl, since the birthday when I had taken her to Disney World for the weekend, back when Mickey Mouse was her whole universe.

❦

THAT NEXT FRIDAY, we didn't do the sex at all. We went straight to the lesson. Emily was there, sitting on the couch. She didn't know any better. She didn't know anything. Still, she was the living, breathing security camera that kept my starlet and I from taking our clothes off and doing what came naturally.

Towards the end of that session, I took a bathroom break, leaving the two of them to chat. As I pissed, I was annoyed that Emily had asked her mother to drop her off early. I knew it was the arrangement I would have to deal with for the immediate future, and that bothered me. I zipped myself up and flushed the toilet. I'd wanted one final taste of that girl, but like so many others, it was over too damn soon.

As I walked across the foyer I could hear them, my girl on piano and Emily singing. Standing on the other side of the closed door, I listened. Emily was singing our starlet's new song, and she was singing it far better than the starlet ever could. I shook my head.

❦

AFTER THE LESSON, I got up and walked down the hill through Boston Common and towards Downtown Crossing. In the Sam Goody music store that was down there, I bought the sheet music to a Britney Spears song, hoping to head this all off. My daughter hated singing for me, hated singing the music that I put before her, but this pop crap—she would give her larynx over to that in a heartbeat. I tried to look at the bright side. At least she was singing at all.

I took the music home and worked all night on it, trying to get it just right. At three-seventeen in the morning, I looked at the clock through hazy eyes and thought it was probably time for bed. I kept at it a bit more and that was the last thing I remembered until I woke up the next morning with an orange blanket draped over me, smiling at my Emily's kindness.

The next two Fridays, the starlet came, flying in from San Francisco and then from Vancouver. Emily was there each time, brimming with excitement, and together the three of us worked to put he finishing touches on our girl's rendition of the song. The final concert of her tour was the next night. It was to be taped for HBO and this was where she would debut her piano playing, for the world to see.

Emily asked our starlet—for she was truly *ours* now, and not just mine—if she would come back to Massachusetts and spend more time with us, learn more songs and such. The starlet gave her a complicated no, explaining that her record label required her to fly out the day after the final show to Sweden and start working with the producers out there on her next album. This made Emily sad.

When the lesson was over, our starlet packed up her bags and handed us two passes to that final show, in case we could fly out. I said we'd see, given it was such short notice. Emily gave our girl an extra long hug and thanked her for everything. What everything was, I'm still not sure of, but I think teenagers are in the habit of thanking people for everything because they never remember the specifics of what people do for them. At least they're trying to be polite, right?

I hugged her as well, then she gave me a kiss on the cheek and she was off. I sat down at the piano and plucked away at some little bit I had been fooling with. Emily sat on the bench beside me.

"I think she likes you, Daddy," Emily informed me, giggling with girlish innuendo. "She kissed you."

"On the cheek, honey. On the cheek."

"Dad, thank you for learning that song."

"Which song, dear?"

"The time you fell asleep. I saw what you were working on and I wanted to say thank you for going to all that effort."

"It's no effort, honey. I love you and if that's the music you want to sing..."

She wrapped her arms around me, stopping my playing. "I love you too, Daddy."

I kissed her forehead. She'd made my day.

Emily rested her head on my shoulder, then asked, "Daddy, can I dye my hair her color?"

THE GIRL WHO ISN'T READY

She sits on the lawn by the lamppost with her baby and her sandwich. Mommy takes generous bites as Baby looks on, wanting what she's having instead of the goop in the glass jar. "I don't want that," Baby would say if she could. "No, get that spoon away from me. I want what you're having."

Baby reaches for the sandwich as her mother takes another bite. Mommy's eyes are on the water and the ducks. She doesn't notice the silent pleas of the child.

The baby moves on, as babies do, inspecting each hair on Mommy's arm individually. She squirms when Mommy wipes away the mixture of spit and snot and apricot paste, her valiant efforts to make some sort of statement with her messy face all in vain.

Oh no. Not the spoon again.

❦

THERE ARE OTHERS TOO, lots of runners trading lunch hours for exercise time. As the Amazon jogs by, I notice the out-of-place shade of orange covering her legs. At first I think nylons, but no, that's not even a possibility, not in the midst of an August heat wave. Self-tanning lotion is the answer. Too cheap to buy the good stuff, the Neutrogena, she went for the generic store brand. I wonder what color her skin will be after another twenty years of using that stuff.

As my eyes follow her, I catch sight of a delicious hunk of man, sitting by himself on a nearby bench. If Fabio is a barometer for female lust, then this is one incredibly hot piece of masculinity. I'm not the only one noticing him. He draws us all into the palm of his hand, like ants to a half-eaten Cadbury egg stolen from Mother's hiding place on Good Friday and dropped into the corner for fear of being caught.

He looks like Sampson in a necktie. Blue shirt, long blonde hair, dark glasses to hide the dark eyes. His legs are crossed in such a way that I pray he does not cross them further. If he does, he might damage those precious family jewels. He clasps his hands on one knee and wears a ring on his thumb, trying to look sophisticated, civilized, trying to hide the beast underneath, the beast in those trousers.

I imagine what he's hiding. I like imagining it. There he is, staring out at the pond, the ducks, just like Mommy, her child, and so many others. Staring. Not a trace of emotion on his face. A trace of sadness maybe? He's annoyed with something? "Come over here honey," I would say to him, if he could hear me. "I'll uncross those legs for you. I'll put a smile on your face. Don't worry. I won't touch the hair."

But who am I kidding? Why would Sampson want the baggage I'm bringing along with me?

⚜

MOMMY OFFERS UP HER BREAST. Perhaps she wasn't being stingy at all. I can't see myself offering my breast to a greedy little child, but that's just me. Maybe if it were cute. Her baby is cute.

She's not exposing herself, but she almost is. And for what? To give Baby what she needs? No, to give Baby what she wants. Baby could get by on milk, or formula, or whatever it is you feed babies, but Mommy's better than that. She wants to give Baby more. You lucked out, Baby. Mommy's breast is better than chicken breast any day of the week

THERE'S a girl by the pond. She leans over. White sleeveless t-shirt. Blue jeans. Little bitty straps to hold all of her in place. Cute, but not too cute. Her beau approaches. Her arms are folded though, beneath her breasts, hiding something, and projecting something at the same time.

He walks away.

Not her beau perhaps? No arm around the shoulder, the waist, the hips, slipping down to have a little feel of her buns through the faded blue jeans. Even more faded now than when she bought them, more faded herself for having found him. He sucks the life from her. Before he came, the geese almost brought a smile to her face. It's gone now.

THE SMELL of gasoline and freshly cut grass reminds me of my own mother, and how she screamed at Dad for his ritual attempt to squeeze that last drop of summer out of an October Saturday. There really wasn't enough grass to warrant a mow, but somehow being out there made him feel the tiniest bit better about the six cold months that lay in front of him.

My baby's not going to have a father. I'm not going to have a husband. No one to yell at for wasting his time mowing the lawn in the rain.

Two more mommies drive their babies by the first mommy, pushing them in carriages, talking to each other like cabbies on the CB, the passengers near invisible, at best props or statements. I bet those babies have to settle for the bottle.

Mommy puts Baby's little pink cap on, and up we go into the little seat slung over Mommy's shoulders. That's a lot better than a silly carriage, don't you think?

How do they see me? How does Sampson see me? My skirt is purple, a flowery and flowy thing, just translucent enough that when I stand by the pond, feeding those lucky duckies, you can almost make out my imperfect little legs. Daddy—not my daddy, but my baby's—he told me once, 'They aren't the legs of a model, but they are gorgeous with all their little flaws.'

I wish he were still here, to hold my hand when they suck her out of me. I'm not ready to offer up my breast yet. I'm sure you would have been a nice baby, but I'm not ready to be Mommy by the lamppost. I'm just not ready.

ACKNOWLEDGEMENTS

The author would like to thank: David Crouse, for your tireless investment in my development as a writer; the members of the workshops I attended at Bradford College, most especially to Heather Davis, Ezekiel Russel, Garry Tardy, Brenda Rubin, Dylan Hall, Erik Paul, and of course, to Joe McGee, for not telling me how to write my story; Pat Vogelpohl for telling me he envied the way I wrote dialogue—you'll never know how much that compliment meant, coming from a writer as talented as you; the staff of the *Bradford ReView,* for letting me lead you for three years, and for occasionally accepting a story of mine; my friends far and wide, all of you, but most especially to Jon, Ken, Stacey, Monica, Mary Ann, Tori, Jimmy, Larsen, Erik, Heather, Greg, Brenda, Rachael, and Tiffany; my parents, Earl and Sue, for always finding a piece of a paper and a pen when I asked for one; my brother, John, for beating his older brother up when we were growing up and keeping me grounded; my grandmother, Josephine, for her love, her stories, and everything else; the rest of my family, for always nodding along when I tried to explain what I was doing with my life; and Stephanie, for telling me to stop it every time I said I was going to give up on this book.

The author would also like to thank Stephen de Jesús Frías for his copyediting work on the second edition.

These stories, some in different form, appeared in *Those Little Bastads*, the first edition of this collection, which, yes, was missing an R in its title. The story behind that is long, and not particularly interesting.

ABOUT THE AUTHOR

E. Christopher Clark is the author of the Stains of Time series, a family saga with a hint of magical realism and a whole lot of time travel. His other books include the short story collections *Out of the Woods* and *Under the World*, the novella *The Seven Wives of Silver*, and a collection of poems cheekily titled *Bad Poetry Night*. His short stories have been published in *Live Free or Ride: Tales of the Concord Coach*, *River Muse: Tales of Lowell & the Merrimack Valley*, and the University of Hawaii's *Vice-Versa*. A graduate of Lesley University's MFA in Creative Writing program, he lives in Massachusetts with his wife and daughters.

echristopherclark.com

facebook.com/eccbooks
x.com/eccbooks
instagram.com/eccbooks
goodreads.com/eccbooks
pinterest.com/eccbooks
amazon.com/E.-Christopher-Clark/e/B00H0G94T0